THE BARN THAT CROWED

2

ANNABELLE SANDLIN

ILLUSTRATED BY: A.R MCKINNEY

Annabelle Sandlin Publications Copyright © 2025
by Annabelle Sandlin
eBook: 978-1-966954-29-3
Paperback: 978-1-966954-32-3
Hardback: 978-1-966954-31-6
LCCN: **2025914991**

CONTENTS

This book is dedicated to my dear friend:

Joyce Arlene Comer
June 30, 1928 – July 24, 2020

When God told me I should write a series of nine books for young readers, Joyce motivated me to write a series for children from eight to the mid-teens.

She and I discussed names and dates for the books. We both fondly remembered 1946, the year after World War II had ended. It was a marvelous time for Joyce, America, and me. Families loved family members, the USA, and especially God.

I loved a picture of an old, faded barn that Joyce had on her living room wall. I told her about a barn two blocks from my home when I was growing up.

I was afraid to walk near that barn because of the many roosters that were so noisy and always looked like they wanted to jump down on me. It was next to ponds in New Richmond, Indiana.

I spent many days on the trunk of a fallen tree, over the water in a pond. I went there to read my Bible and to write poems that I gave to many people. Thus, God gave me the series title, "The Barn that Crowed."

Joyce asked that I name one of the leading characters Joyce and her mother, Iris Belle, after her and her mother. I named Amanda after my beautiful great-granddaughter.

MEETING THE TEAM

Amanda Martin, a tomboy, was the beautiful, ten years old daughter of *Betty and John Martin*. Her brother, *Jimmy Martin,* was two years older. Amanda's best friend was *Joyce Perkin*s, who lived next door. Jimmy's best friend was *Bob Perkins*, Joyce's twin brother. Amanda and Jimmy were both tall and had red hair. Both kids were very smart; Amanda was going into the sixth grade but would attend Math and English classes in the high school. She was considered the smartest student in the Merrysville Public School. *Jimmy* attended Junior High and was in the eighth grade. He attended History and Math classes with high school students.

The Martin family owned the *Martin Gardens* and grew vegetables for Kroger and Piggly Wiggly, the two largest grocery chains in the United States in 1946. Betty raised flowers and hired local women to make clothes, aprons, and crafts. Summer was a busy time for the Martin family and their employees.

The Martin family hired most of the local high school and a few junior high school students to work part-time in their gardens and orchards after school in the spring and fall, and for no more than thirty hours a week in the summer. Every day their supervisor, *Frank Johnson,* visits each site and talks to each worker. *Betty Martin* would bring water or Kool-Aid to each site every morning and afternoon. They treated everyone so fairly that all the kids wanted to work in their gardens and orchards, year after year.

John Martin loved to wear bib overalls.

Jimmy and Amanda worked a few hours a week at the Gardens. So did their friends Joyce and Bob Perkins.

While the boys fished and accused the girls of spending all their time playing with dolls, the girls spent many hours at The Barn that Crowed. They helped *Sheriff Webb* solve some serious crimes. The sheriff and the girls' mothers were the only people who knew of their talent. *Betty Martin and Iris Belle Perkins* were great bakers, cooks, and seamstresses. Their food and other items were in much demand.

Joyce and Bob Perkins were the twin children of *Art and Iris Belle Perkins*. Ten years old Joyce was short, had long blonde ringlets, and had blue eyes like her beautiful mother. She always dressed in beautiful clothes given to her by her rich grandmother. No blue jeans or casual slacks for Joyce. Bob was tall and had hazel eyes like his dad. No one could tell they were twins.

Joyce's dad, *Arthur (Art) Perkins*, owned many successful real estate and insurance businesses. He always wore a suit. He did a lot of his work from his office that was located on the side entrance to their lovely home. There was usually a lot of traffic coming into their driveway with customers and staff checking in.

Other people you'll read about in the *Barn That Crowed* books include:

Andrew Spitznaugle (Mr. Andy)—Mr. Andy's grandparents inherited the land that the residents of the village of Merrysville now occupied. There were acres of gravel when his parents and grandparents first arrived. They started a business making bricks out of the gravel and selling gravel to contractors. After the brick factory burned, his family began building houses, roads, and businesses. They sold the land by acreage into farms, businesses, and residential lots. They became very rich. Fortunately, they were generous people who wanted to see their land become a nice town.

The Spitznaugle family donated land and had two grain elevators built next to the railroad tracks, so the local farmers had a means to market their harvest. He and three friends owned one elevator, while the other was owned and maintained by a co-op of many farmers for miles around.

Mr. Andy's two farms were the biggest users of his elevator. The trains took the grain to be made into flour, cereal, animal feed, and many other markets.

The removal of the gravel had produced three very deep gravel pits, which the village called the Merrysville Ponds. A fish hatchery in Canada had sold three truckloads of fish to a company in Kentucky that could not take them because of a bad leak. They met Andy's dad at the gas station and told him they needed to dump the fish somewhere. They gave them to Mr. Andy's dad when he offered to allow them to dump them into his deepest pond.

Mr. Andy and his father developed the ponds and the land around them into a beautiful village park. They donated the park, with tennis courts, a picnic area, a square dance building, parking lots, and extra land for the village to enjoy.

His family had the roads and city streets built. They had a nice cemetery built outside of town.

The village had no name in 1926. Not wanting to call it Spitznaugle, Mr. Andy's eight-year-old daughter told her best friend that this village was Merrysville. When her grandparents heard her, they loved it and had it officially incorporated as Merrysville.

Martha and David Rosenbaum and Benji – A Jewish family who recently moved into a lovely home in Merrysville. Their 10-year-old son, Benji, is a friend of Jimmy and Bob's. ***David*** is president of a company that sells to the US military. ***Martha*** makes delicious bagels and bagel spreads.

Sam and Tanya Hanaway, and Jason –Their 10-year-old son, ***Jason***, is a friend of Jimmy and Bob's- ***Sam*** is a pharmacist; ***Tanya*** will be teaching French in the Merrysville school.

Mr. and Mrs. Butler and their 10-year-old son, ***Chris Butler.*** – ***Mr. Butler*** owns the local hardware store. ***Mrs. Butler*** is a hairdresser.

Abby, Nellie, and Phyllis – Girlfriends of Amanda and Joyce. Abby's parents were killed in a car accident, so she lives with her sister and grandparents.

Frank Johnson – A veteran who came to get a meal for working. He did many repairs and painted the Martin home before being hired to be supervisor of the Martin Gardens.

Mel and Phyllis Jones – Owners of the grocery store.

Ellis Sandlin – Famous singer and brother of Phyllis Jones

Sheriff Webb – The county sheriff and friend of the Martin and Perkins families.

PROLOGUE

THE WEEK AFTER MEMORIAL DAY

School in Merrysville, Indiana, was out for the summer just a few weeks ago. Amanda and Jimmy Martin, Bob and Joyce Perkins, and other friends had used the first day to visit a barn nearby and other fun places. They met Mr. Andy, the owner of the barn, and became friends of that barn. The first thing the kids saw when they went into the barn was the sign, "Welcome to the Barn that Crows."

Life seemed quiet in Merrysville over the weekend following the holiday celebrations on Thursday, May 30, 1946. The holiday, known by some as Decoration Day and others as Memorial Day, had been special because the village of Merrysville celebrated its fiftieth anniversary by the unveiling of beautiful new village signs in the morning and fireworks in the park that evening. A huge carnival was in town for eight days. There were probably three thousand people from neighboring villages, cities, and farms attending part or most of the celebrations in Merrysville. In a village of fourteen hundred residents, the village was crowded. Cars everywhere! Food! Food! Food! The fireworks were the best in the United States.

George Price, the older brother of Joe Price, the Town Marshal of Merrysville, and John Price, the caretaker of the cemetery, had been arrested just days before the Memorial Day celebration. He had killed two men. His attorney was defending him as temporarily insane. He refused to let his brothers visit him in jail. Amanda and Joyce had brought the murder to the sheriff's attention. Only the sheriff and their mothers knew how the girls had solved the crime.

The Martins and Perkins had a large potluck party and square dance in the Martin backyard on the evening of Thursday, May 30, 1946. They grilled hamburgers, hot dogs, and fresh fish caught by several of the boys attending the party. There were more than forty children and their families attending. There were all kinds of games, prizes, and food. Parents were able to meet the friends of their children.

The fabulous fireworks at the park seemed to explode in full glory in the sky over the Martin yard. Everyone felt they had a better view of the fireworks at the party than the crowd watching at the park.

Nearly every guest who attended the Martin/Perkins Memorial Day 1946 party on Thursday evening slept in on Friday morning. After all, everyone stayed until one a.m.

Of course, Mel and Phyllis Jones, the owners of the Merrysville Grocery Store, opened the store at 7 a.m., the same as any other Friday morning. Six hours earlier they were the last family to say, "Thanks for a great evening."

Every customer was curious about what happened at the Martin/ Perkins party on Memorial Day. Most customers had driven by and seen the party of more than 100 happy people, or they had been at the park where they heard many wonderful sounds from the Martin back yard, four blocks away.

Customers learned that the party was attended by the families of nine-to-twelve-year-old friends of the Martin/Perkins children. David and Martha Rosenbaum, Merrysville's newest residents, were there with their ten-year old son, Benji. Customers learned that Martha Rosenbaum had baked more than 150 bagels and made the delicious toppings for the bagels. Phyllis Jones told her customers the bagels and toppings were outstanding. She had learned a lot about the Jewish faith and the millions of Jews and other people killed during the Holocaust that happened during World War Two.

Every person in town was surprised to learn the hit of the Martin/ Perkins party had been the fifty-minute concert by famous singer Ellis Sandlin, accompanied by five of his singers. They were a big part of the program. They were surprised to learn that Ellis Sandlin is Phyllis Jones' brother. Most customers wanted to know what songs Ellis sang and what fun things he did on stage. All the customers let Phyllis know how wonderful the concert sounded at the park.

Mr. Andy, the Mayor of Merrysville, hosted the morning New Sign unveiling and Merrysville History program, but did not attend the evening fireworks service in the park. Instead, he attended the Martin/Perkins party.

The customers learned that Mr. Andy attended because he will be teaching these children in Sunday school, starting this fall. Mr. Andy had a story of the village history printed and distributed at the dedication of the beautiful new **Welcome to Merrysville** signs.

On Friday, May 31st, Mr. Andy fed his animals in the Barn that Crows. He collected the eggs and took them to the grocery store like he had for years. Many kids in town were scheduled to take tennis lessons from Mr. Andy during the day on Mondays, Wednesdays, and Fridays. Many parents were scheduled to start lessons with him in the evenings. Phyllis Jones encouraged parents to call Mr. Andy and schedule lessons so they could participate in the parent vs children tennis tournament that Mr. Andy was planning to host before winter. He hopes to make this an annual event.

The carnival, that covered six blocks on the Merrysville streets downtown for eight days, closed at midnight on Saturday, June 1st, and had been dismantled and moved to their next site. All the clutter and debris had been cleaned from the streets as soon as they left. Sunday was church as usual.

Chapter 1

The Week Begins

The first thing anyone in the Martin and Perkins' households heard on Monday after the holiday was, of course, the roosters who lived in the upstairs window of The Barn That Crowed. Amanda smiled as she got out of bed and stretched. Her friend Joyce had spent the night and was fast asleep. Amanda and Joyce could hardly wait to feed a snack to the roosters when they were able to go to the barn. Those roosters were so gentle and friendly since they got to know the girls.

They loved the chickenfeed the girls fed them. Amanda hoped there would be no visitors in the barn after their tennis lessons and practice today so they could go in. If the coast was clear, they planned to spend an hour or so in their hideout.

There it was again! Amanda made a funny face at her reflection in the mirror, stuck her tongue out at the funny face, then brushed her teeth. After she had dressed and washed her face and hands, Amanda followed the compelling aroma of bacon, drifting through the hallway from the kitchen.

-   -   -   -   -   -   -   -   -   -   -   -

Chapter 2

Wolves

Cock-a-doodle-doo! Cock-a-doodle-doo!

When she came into the kitchen, Amanda saw her mother looking out the dining room window. Amanda thought her mother was watching the many birds eating at the birdfeeders in the yard. Not true. For some reason, there were no birds feeding.

When she heard Amanda, Betty turned around and suggested that Amanda look out the window at a huge turkey buzzard in their yard, picking up a dead rabbit.

Betty Martin had a frown on her face. Neither the mother nor the daughter had ever seen a turkey buzzard up close. A large black crow was trying his best to get his share of the rabbit, to no avail. Betty told Amanda she was trying to figure out how a rabbit could die in their back yard.

Amanda was aghast at the scene she saw and started to cry. Betty put her arm around her daughter's shoulder and kissed her cheek. Suddenly they saw a young wolf run out from behind a bush next to the fence.It appeared that it killed the rabbit, then had been frightened by the huge turkey buzzard.

While the crow was left standing, the buzzard smugly flew off with the rabbit. With his head down and tail between his legs, the young wolf left the yard and quickly ran toward the gardens where the wolf den was located under the big barn.

Amanda and Betty knew that Mr. Martin needed to have the wolves moved.

Amanda quickly followed Betty when she ran toward the thick growth of low bushes. Amanda heard the sigh of relief coming from Betty when she confirmed the two killdeer birds were alive. The female was sitting on the nest of eggs while the male was standing guard next to the nest. Betty assured Amanda that everything was fine, then she ran inside and called her husband.

John was flabbergasted when Betty told him about the shock of seeing a wolf in their back yard. He was grateful that the buzzard had seen the wolf attack the rabbit and scared it back to the den.

John felt bad that he had not done something a few months ago when he saw a young wolf under the Shipping Barn. At the time, he felt the young wolf had stopped at the barn on its way through the area. John hadn't heard of another wolf being spotted in that county for forty years.

John quickly called a company in Lafayette that specialized in relocating animals. They were surprised about wolves in the Merrysville area. Many of their employees were at the barn before noon. They explained that these wolves will be very welcome in the northern Michigan forests where the overabundance of deer and other wild animals was causing many auto accidents as the deer crossed the roads in herds. Deer had also been dying of starvation, and birth defects had been found in many animals.

The workers had on white uniforms and gas masks. They put a sleeping-gas tank into the opening under the floor of the building. In just minutes, the workers were quickly under the building. There was plenty of space for the men to crawl into the large den and hand out the sleeping wolves to other workers. The wolves were still asleep when they were carefully placed into the back of the large, enclosed truck bed.

When John had gotten the call from Betty, he still thought there were only a few wolf pups and their mother under the barn. Soon, it was obvious that many wolf families traveled and lived together. There were many more babies and young wolves than the workers from Lafayette expected. Many adults were living there as well.

John Martin and Frank Johnson were amazed as they watched the wolves being carefully removed from their den. The supervisor of the removal team was grateful that he had brought many workers.

John and Frank discussed how beautiful and healthy the animals were. None were unhealthy; none were skinny. Neither man said anything, but both were wondering how many rabbits and rodents it took to feed a menagerie this large. In a short time, all the wolves were safely in the huge truck.

The large glass door was safely shut and locked so John and Frank could see how carefully the wolves had been placed on packing blankets. They felt bad because they could see that the wolves were frightened and shivering as they awoke. It was nice to see how the adult wolves quickly reunited with their young, comforting them as a family unit, in the truck.

By that evening, after a long ride, the beautiful but scared wolves would be in their new home in a Michigan forest. In a few days, they would have selected a sight for the den that would house their families.

When the truck pulled away, John immediately had some of his maintenance men prepare the back of that barn with a cement wall, having a foundation going very deep so no animal would ever claim that area again.

Knowing that the wolves were safely off the property was a relief to Frank Johnson, the Martin Gardens' supervisor. Frank shivered when he silently thanked God that he had chosen to live in Amanda's playhouse instead of living in that barn. When John Martin had told him about seeing wolves, he really thought it was a joke.

Most of the school children in Merrysville, Indiana, had part-time jobs. They had been working in the fields since school was out over three weeks ago. In the gardens, carrots, lettuce, spinach, green onions, and radishes were harvested, cleaned, and taken to Kroger and Piggly Wiggly stores. Tomatoes were growing, corn and potatoes were up, strawberries and black raspberries were nearly ready for picking, and the bees had already made a lot of clover honey. Yes, life in Merrysville was getting back to normal.

Last week, Frank and the garden workers who picked and cleaned vegetables didn't know the wolves were under the barn where they worked. John and Frank were grateful that no wolf had ever come into the barn or fields.

Chapter 3

Free Movies, Social Time
in Merrysville

In 1946, many small towns and villages had no planned social life for its residents. Fortunately, Merrysville had something planned for at least once or twice a month. It seemed like there was always something going on at, or being planned for, the park or downtown.

Everyone looked forward to the week after Memorial Day. Adults and kids alike could hardly wait to get together for the free movies. It was good for the farmers, store owners, and every person in town.

Every Tuesday, Thursday, and Saturday nights, free movies were shown on the large side wall of the hardware store on one of the side streets downtown. Farmers and residents of neighboring towns and villages came from miles around to watch the Shirley Temple, Tarzan, Lone Ranger, Sherlock Holmes, Lassie, Little Orphan Annie, and movies starring Humphrey Bogart, Betty Grable, Clark Gable, Spencer Tracy and so many other stars.

A short movie for younger viewers was always shown first, then the main feature. There was a fifteen minute break when the projectionist changed reels. Amanda and Joyce's favorite movies were Shirley Temple and Little Orphan Annie. Their brothers liked Lassie and Tarzan movies. Everyone had to bring a chair or a blanket to sit on, on the pavement.

©Annabelle Sandlin

Their parents brought their folding chairs and sat behind their children and their friends who were sitting on the blankets they brought. Kids had such fun talking to their friends who also sat on blankets near their families.

The Martin and Perkins family arrived around 8 p.m. Shortly after that, the street was full of people. The movies didn't start until it was dark, so kids and adults were able to visit with many friends before the movie began.

Many of the girls and boys who saw each other at school lived quite a distance from each other. Getting to see each other three times a week gave them a chance to tell each other all that was happening in their lives. Amanda and Joyce had six other girls who shared their big blanket on the pavement. Jimmy and Bob took turns sitting on some of their classmates' blankets. The nice thing about the sharing, the blankets were in front of someone's parents, so they also shared stories about their kids. It was definitely a favorite time for everyone.

Five cent and ten cent bags of popcorn were available from six to ten p.m. from different businesses. The drugstore was very busy selling ten cent cherry or chocolate cokes, or fifteen cent milkshakes. Most stores selling food were offering hamburgers for fifteen cents, and hot dogs for ten cents. It was a nickel more if you added cheese and pickle relish. It was a great time for visiting with friends and family.

Many couples who didn't have a car considered these free movies as their dates. Many married couples said the movies were where they met and dated. A hamburger and drink while sitting and watching the free movies was just as exciting as going to a drive-in theatre, and more reasonable. Most of the feature films had been shown at a theatre the year before, but no one cared. Many of the featured films were much older.

When the show ended, family members met at a planned location for the walk or drive home. Most of the movies were carefully chosen for this crowd by the Township Council.

The stores sold groceries, hardware, clothing, and other items until they closed an hour after the movies were over. For many stores, sales on the three months of movie nights provided more than fifty percent of their annual sales.

Time before and after the movies provided many families with their only social life. These were the only movies many local and neighboring residents had the opportunity to watch. They gave people something in common to talk and laugh about. Yes, the movies were good for all the people of Merrysville

Chapter 4

The Blessings at the Barn

Amanda and Joyce made sure they were visiting the Barn that Crows nearly every day. Today, about an hour after a train stopped for water, the girls heard two men coming in to see what the barn was like. The men were pleased at the cleanliness and kindness seen in the barn.

The girls heard the men talk about changing the clothes they wore when they were on the straw in the train car. One man said something, and both men laughed, A few minutes later, after the barn door closed, Amanda quietly whispered and asked Joyce what the man said. Joyce told Amanda that the man said, "We'll leave our knapsacks in the barn while we go and, hopefully, find someone to feed us."

The men walked around the driveway to the front of the building toward the exit. **Cock-a-doodle-doo! Cock-a-doodle-doo!**

Sounds of the men screaming at the roosters allowed the girls to know that the men were on the path under the barn window that the roosters claimed as their territory. The men walked around the driveway to the front of the building toward the exit. The girls looked at each other and laughed.

They could remember how they felt when they were facing the roosters just weeks ago. Amanda laughed and said, "Joyce, I am so glad that the roosters change their tone when we're within their sight." Joyce laughed and said, "Me, too, Amanda. What I think is funny, is, that every time the boys are with us, they think the roosters are nice because they like the boys." Both girls laughed again.

The girls were already naming some of those roosters. They quickly seemed to know their names. The girls hurried to feed and talk to their pets. The girls were especially thrilled at the feel of the roosters' beaks as some of them ate the special feed out of their hands. Amanda smiled at a rooster and told him, "When you trust me to feed you out of my hand, it gives me the warm fuzzies." Joyce turned around and said, "That's how I feel, too."

Cock-a-doodle-doo! Cock-a-doodle-doo! It had been over an hour ago when the roosters first spotted those two men. The men were laughing as they were returning down the driveway. Amanda and Joyce quickly retreated to their hideout.

Both men were elated when they quickly returned to the area where they had left their knapsacks. The joy of the men resounded in the barn. It made the girls smile at each other.

The girls learned that as soon as the men had left the park, they ate at the first house outside the park. As they ate, the men told the couple that they had gone to the grain elevator across the tracks before going into the barn. They had an interview lined up in an hour. As they ate, the couple told the men what a great place the grain elevators were to work.

"With farm equipment being manufactured once again, most farmers are farming more acreage, thus sending more grain on trains from the elevators. Also, several elevator employees who planned to retire several years ago, just retired this year and are moving to Florida. They had worked several more years before retiring because younger men were in the war, and the elevators couldn't hire anyone to replace them. Their houses will probably be up for sale before winter in case you're interested."

After eating, the men had interviewed at the grain elevator, and were hired for the jobs they wanted. They hurried back to the barn to change back into their old clothes they had worn on the empty train car. They started to work in an hour.

The men sounded so happy as they were planning to stay in the barn for a week or so until they could find some permanent housing. They were praising God and talking about how pleased they were about seeing the church downtown when they first arrived. One of the men said he was going to borrow enough money from someone to call home that evening and tell his wife to plan to move when he found the housing and received his first paycheck. The men were whistling "Onward Christian Soldiers" as they ran out of the barn and headed across the railroad tracks to their new jobs.

The girls were thrilled when they heard them whistling a Christian hymn. Amanda asked Joyce, "Were you surprised last month when our choir director said that song was written in 1871?" Joyce nodded and said, "I was." The girls left the barn smiling after saying goodbye to their roosters.

Amanda and Joyce went to their homes to tell their mothers everything they had heard the men talking about. The mothers were happy to hear that those two Christian men got the jobs and were looking forward to attending church on Sunday.

That evening, the two men came to the Martin house to see if they could do something to earn a meal. When John and Betty heard them talking about the joy of their new jobs, they invited the men to eat at their house every night until they got their first paycheck next week. John suggested each of the men was welcome to use the Martin phone to call his wife to let her know they had gotten the job. The Martin's were told that both wives could hardly wait to move to such a wonderful town.

When Joyce told her mother about the men, she told Joyce that she and her dad would invite them to come eat with them. When Amanda told her about her parents inviting them to eat with their family, Iris Belle talked to Betty about having the men alternate eating at the two homes for meals until they had the money to eat out. If they did, the men would know four members from church to introduce to their families when they arrived.

Early the next morning, the men met Mr. Andy when he came in to feed his animals. They told him about two church families that had invited them to be their guests for supper until they have a paycheck. They told him they intend to attend the church with the two families this Sunday. Mr. Andy told them what nice people the Martins and Perkins are. They also learned that Mr. Andy attended the same church. He told them that he would put some groceries in the refrigerator so they could fix their breakfast before they went to work.

He mentioned that he would make sure they had many fresh eggs from his hens. The men knew their families were going to be blessed in Merrysville.

Chapter 5

Special Deed for June

What a fun time the girls had taking lessons and playing great tennis for three hours. They realized that Mr. Andy was a great tennis teacher. He was thrilled at the talent the two girls showed on the court. The other six girls who took lessons at the same time seemed to enjoy the lessons but were not as enthusiastic about learning the game. It appeared to Mr. Andy that tennis was just their opportunity to spend time with Amanda and Joyce.

Mr. Andy believed that he could help make Joyce and Amanda into the champions that they could be if they chose. He knew they would be playing tennis in college. He also believed he would be teaching Amanda and Joyce tennis for several more years and one or both girls would be good enough to qualify to go professional. After two hours of lessons and an extra game of couples, all eight girls were exhausted and went to their separate homes.

Amanda and her family were finishing their supper when Betty Martin made an announcement, "Tomorrow evening we will have fresh baked black raspberry cobbler for dessert, thanks to Jimmy and Amanda. That is, if you two are willing to go down to Mrs. Hall's house tomorrow to help her."

"Amanda, you and Joyce were looking for something special you could do for someone in June. Well, Mrs. Hall called today to say that she has many ripe black raspberries that need to be picked soon. She informed me that last year she was sick, and all berries that were not eaten by the birds, rotted on the bushes."

"I felt bad that no one was aware that her berries were not being picked. I promised her that you could pick them, and I would make her pies. The berries ripen every day for about a month, so you can pick them early every morning before the birds get them. Mrs. Hall insisted that I also make pies for us whenever you could find time to pick the berries. I also plan to surprise her by making many jars of raspberry jams and jellies for her to have this winter with her peanut butter sandwiches."

"Jimmy, she said to tell you that she has a problem that she thinks you could eliminate. Somehow, one or two of her venetian blinds came down and need to be rehung. She has a ladder, so we don't need to take ours."

"I know she appreciates all that you two do for her. She tells everyone what a great help you are, and what a professional job you do on her lawn. Thank you, Amanda for taking her food and giving her back and neck massages when you are there. Thanks, both of you, for being so special. You two make me so proud of your loving spirits."

Both kids loved doing things for Mrs. Hall. She had such great stories to tell them about her life in the nineteenth century in Canada before her family moved to the United States.

They learned everything she and her family had to do to become American citizens. Both kids shared many of her stories in classes at school.

Jimmy and Amanda each chose two large containers to carry the berries home after they had completed any other jobs that needed to be done. Betty handed Amanda a pint size container and told her, "Always fill this container and leave it with Mrs. Hall to have with her cereal."

Amanda could hardly believe all the berries that were ripe. She picked nearly three full containers while Jimmy was inside hanging venetian blinds. Two times Amanda had to scare away some crows who were hoping to have the black raspberries for dinner.

Jimmy was surprised when he saw a full container of berries sitting at the end of one of the rows. When he and Amanda finished picking the last of the berries, Jimmy whistled and told Amanda, "Wow! This year is going to be a bumper crop. I wonder if our berries will be this good. Our kitchen is going to see a lot of baking."

Amanda laughed and replied, "I've just been thinking about all the jam and jelly Mrs. Hall will have this winter to eat with her peanut butter sandwiches that she likes so much. She's going to love Mom." Jimmy smiled and added, "And, you and Joyce for picking the berries." When the kids went inside, Mrs. Hall was thrilled to have the pint of fresh berries that Amanda handed her.

When they hugged Mrs. Hall and told her goodbye, she said, "Why don't you two consider taking a shortcut through my pasture? You may see Mr. Mason's milk cow and his granddaughter's two ponies. They usually stay down at the other end of the pasture. If they see you two, they may come down to be petted."

"There is a stile at the end of the fence that is next to your school ball fields. You can climb over the stile, into the schoolyard. It would save you over two blocks to get home with those heavy containers of berries." The kids thought that was a great idea and went through her gate into the pasture.

After Amanda had climbed over the stile, Jimmy handed the berries to her. She carefully placed the heavy buckets of berries on the ground to wait for Jimmy to come down from the stile. Jimmy put his right hand up and was busily waving at someone. Amanda turned around to see who had Jimmy's attention.

She saw several of his friends standing near the school baseball field, waving, and motioning for Jimmy to join them. Jimmy was standing still on the top step of the stile when Amanda turned around and screamed, "Jimmy, quick, get down from the stile. Mr. Mason's bull is coming toward you. Hurry!" And hurry he did.

Jimmy hadn't jumped two steps away from the stile when, going as fast as the bull's legs would carry him, the bull aimed one of his horns straight at that stile. The fence shook as the stile was lifted into the air, and a loud thud as it returned to the ground. The noisy thud convinced all the kids that the bull was not playing. Jimmy's friends were running as fast as they could to check on him and Mrs. Hall's stile.

Jimmy laughed and said, "I should have thought about what Mrs. Hall told me earlier inside the house. She mentioned Mr. Mason had a bull. As we were leaving, she said that Mr. Mason had rented the pasture for his granddaughter's horses and his milk cow. We all know that Mrs. Hall's eyesight isn't very good. If she saw the bull grazing in her pasture, she must have thought it was a milk cow, not a bull." Jimmy's friends laughed and then went back to the ball field to continue their game.

The bull, snorting and stomping, stared at the kids, hit the stile once again with its horn, snorted, turned around, and leisurely headed toward Mr. Mason's barn. Both kids sat down for a few minutes to catch their breath before heading home. They agreed that they would not take any more shortcuts through Mrs. Hall's pasture.

After hearing the bull story, Betty Martin called Mr. Mason and related how the stile was damaged. He and Betty Martin laughed but agreed the incident could have been a horror story. Mr. Mason thanked Betty for the call and said he would get the bull in the barn and repair the stile immediately so it would be safe to be used. Betty assured him that it would never be used by her kids.

Later Amanda talked to Joyce and their moms about picking the black raspberries. Betty suggested the girls would need to be busy early every morning for about four weeks. This would be their June volunteer gift to Mrs. Hall. Both Joyce and her mother thought it was a great idea. No one was smiling when Joyce started a discussion of the special deed done for May. All four were hoping June would be better.

Iris Belle suggested it would be easier on the girls to take four buckets instead of two. Since there were so many berries, they could carry less in each bucket and use both hands. Betty Martin laughed and told Iris Belle that they had carried four large buckets that day. Betty insisted that Joyce must keep one of the buckets for their family. That pleased Joyce and Iris Belle. They could almost taste the pies they knew Iris Belle would soon be baking.

The Martin Garden berries would be ripe in a few weeks. Until then, Betty would bake pies for her family and Mrs. Hall. She would freeze many pies she made from Mrs. Hall's berries. She felt sure that she would bake enough pies that Mrs. Hall could have one pie every two weeks during the winter months. Betty was surprised yesterday by the huge number of berries there are this year. She also would be able to make Mrs. Hall many jars of jam and jelly from the berries in her orchard.

Mrs. Martin baked three pies and made several small canning jars of jelly with the large number of berries the children picked. She stored most of the jars of jelly in the box that the canning jars came in.

Early the next morning, Betty Martin drove two girls, one jar of jelly, and a huge fourteen-inch black raspberry pie to Mrs. Hall's house. Mrs. Hall looked at the pie and said, "Betty Martin, I have never seen such a big pie before." Betty laughed and told her she could share it with her neighbors.

Amanda, of course, told the bull and stile story in such a dramatic way that all four of them had a big laugh. Mrs. Hall wanted to cut the pie so she could share it with Betty, Amanda, and Joyce, but Betty let her know that she had made two pies for her family.

When Betty shared that Joyce's family would also get enough berries to keep them in pies, Mrs. Hall's face lit up in a smile, and she told Joyce that made her very happy.

Mrs. Hall was pleased when Amanda told her how her family members were thanking her last night at supper when they ate their first black raspberry pie of the season.

When Amanda finished telling of the experience in the pasture, Mrs. Hall said, "Oh, I do remember now that Mr. Mason told me when he bought a new bull. My eyesight isn't what it used to be, so I hadn't noticed a bull in the pasture. It looked like a milk cow to me." Everyone laughed, including Mrs. Hall. "Now Betty Martin, you keep most of those berries for your family. Maybe in a week or two, when you bake a pie for your family, you would be kind enough to make one for me also." Betty assured her that she would have many raspberry pies that summer.

Betty told Mrs. Hall, "We have a raspberry patch as well. The berries are still small and green, so we should have berries in three to five weeks, about the time your raspberries are done for the season. Your berries grow and ripen quicker because they receive full sun since they are next to the open barnyard." As she was closing the screen door, Amanda noticed that Mrs. Hall already had a saucer and fork on the table and was smiling as she cut herself a large slice of her first black raspberry pie of the season.

Every morning the girls got up early, ate, and walked the mile to Mrs. Hall's raspberry patch. When Mrs. Hall joined them for a short while in the berry patch, the three females would stand and talk, pigging out on the berries as they shared the news of the day. Joyce often told Amanda, "I really feel blessed to have gotten to know Mrs. Hall so well. I feel like I have a new friend. I will be sharing some of her experiences at school. Our class always liked her stories that you shared."

Three days a week, for over a month, Mrs. Hall had a fresh raspberry pie delivered to her by Amanda when she and Joyce came to pick the berries. Mrs. Hall told the girls that she was inviting her neighbors to come and eat the pies with her. Daily she also shared part of the pint of fresh berries. It seemed she was becoming popular in the neighborhood because of those berries and pies.

Mrs. Hall still had no idea that Betty Martin was making jams and jellies for her. Amanda and Joyce knew the treats would assure that Mrs. Hall would eat well that winter. Every Friday, Betty also sent a jar of the raspberry jelly with Mrs. Hall's pie. Mrs. Hall's eyes danced when she reminded the girls often of how she loved the black raspberry jelly with her peanut butter sandwiches.

Chapter 6

Murder Overheard

One afternoon after their chores were done, Joyce and Amanda were in their hideout when the 2 p.m. train from Chicago slowed down for water.

Twenty minutes later they heard voices of two men coming into the barn. The girls were scared and kept very quiet. Two men that came to Merrysville last week were so cheerful and singing Christian songs.

These two men were just the opposite. They were talking about a man that one of them had mugged and possibly killed in a suburb of Chicago. They sounded like they were arguing.

One man was convinced that someone could identify them. The other man reminded him, "Hey, quit your bellyaching. That city is nearly sixty miles from our homes. Neither of us knows anyone in that town anyway, so if that woman did see us in the dark, she couldn't identify us. Neither of us has ever been arrested, so there wouldn't be any mug shots of us for her to identify. We didn't leave any fingerprints."

The other man did not sound convinced when he answered, "What? No fingerprints? You're kidding yourself. You hit him with that big rock and just threw the rock down beside him. It had to have your fingerprints and the man's blood on it. You didn't wipe it off before you threw it down. I just don't feel comfortable about it. It wasn't right and you know it." Both girls realized the danger they were in if they were discovered. Neither girl so much as whispered.

©Annabelle Sandlin

The girls heard the first man snap at the other, "Quit your bellyaching. Get control of yourself. I think I threw the rock behind the tree. They won't see it. Just forget it ever happened. You've got to. I'm hungry; you must be as well. Come on, let's go into Merrysville to see if we're able to get someone to feed us. We can't be seen eating and paying with this much money. The man handed you a ten-dollar bill, but everything I grabbed out of his pocket were twenty-dollar bills. It might look suspicious even if we use the ten-dollar bill."

The short man was sincere, when he nearly whispered, "Try to excuse yourself if you want, but as far as I'm concerned, I'll never forget that I left him there bleeding. It's blood money. I don't ever want to eat anything you pay for with that money."

"If you are that worried, maybe we should stay put for a few weeks while you calm down. I don't know what we'll do with the money. I'm sorry. I still can't believe I was that stupid."

"I call it greedy," was the response of the short man. "And stupid as well."

"Look at the nice cots and blankets on the shelves on the wall. This place has water and a toilet. It's nice and clean. We could plan to live in this barn if we keep it clean. It's so much better than the corncob shed behind that elevator we went to before we came over here."

"Now, come on. You've got to calm down. Let's go see if we can find someone to feed us supper." The girls heard the weak reply, "OK, let's go." The barn door slammed shut behind the men.

Only moments later, a truck pulled up. Someone got out and came into the barn after the two men were a block away. The girls didn't hear Mr. Andy when he climbed the stairs or as he filled several water jars and put some chicken feed into the troughs.

He poured cream for the cats and kittens that occupied the first floor. Mr. Andy had not said a word, so it was after he fed the roosters, and told his cats goodnight that the girls recognized who was in the barn with them.

They looked at each other and quietly said, "Let's go tell Mr. Andy what we heard." Joyce yelled, "Mr. Andy, we have something to tell you." No answer. They were not aware that he had gone out the door, driven around the barn, through the park, and was on his way home by the time the girls had closed their hideout. They quickly climbed down from the haymow, and exited the door running, hoping to catch him. The girls knew they missed him when they saw the taillights of his red truck as it left the park driveway.

Joyce and Amanda ran down the hidden pathway where the strangers would not be able to see them. "What should we do, Joyce? I know I need to quickly write down everything I heard or I'll forget something when I'm telling Mother." Joyce answered, "I think we need to tell our mothers and dads. Maybe we should call our friend, Sheriff Webb. No, I agree with you; we need to write everything down before we forget something important."

As they turned the corner by their houses, their brothers were sitting on the bench, cleaning their fish on the picnic table. Each girl headed for her house. The boys asked the girls where they were going. Neither girl wanted her brother to come in when she was talking to her mother about what they had heard. They were very scared but told the boys that they were going to their bedrooms. Each girl went directly to her bedroom to write down every detail that they remembered and pray about the situation.

Amanda had just gone to her room when she heard the boys talking to someone. Minutes later, there was a knock on the back door. The two men stood there, asking Betty Martin if they could mow the lawn and cut some wood for a meal. She told them, "The lawnmower is by the barn, and one of you could trim around the flowers while the other mows." In her room, Amanda immediately recognized the two voices. She knew she needed to talk to her mother when Jimmy would not be coming in with his fish.

When Betty Martin heard the men coming to tell her they had finished working, she quickly took some of the freshly baked bread and placed it, with two large slices of meatloaf, on each plate.

The men were near the front porch when Betty handed each of them the plates that also contained mashed potatoes with gravy, and fresh vegetables.

The men were sitting on two lawn chairs when Betty took a tall glass of lemonade with chunks of ice for each of the men. The men were finishing the food when John Martin pulled into the driveway. Betty had John take out dessert for the men. They were appreciative and told him how lucky he was to have a wife who was so nice, and such a good cook. John agreed with the men.

They talked for a few minutes about the possibility of new jobs in the area. Amanda was listening to their every word from behind the curtains of her open bedroom window. She was shocked when the men lied and told John they had just arrived from their homes in Philadelphia.

When she heard that, she quickly exited the back door and ran over to tell Joyce that the bad men were in her front yard. When she saw Joyce at her table eating supper, Amanda returned home and to her room, visibly shaken. The men were gone but she could hear her mother and dad talking. She heard her dad telling the boys to grab a ball and gloves so they could play catch in the back yard. Amanda heard Betty and Iris Belle sitting on the bench outside, talking.

Amanda made herself a meatloaf sandwich and went back into her bedroom. She read her notes, then remembered another sentence of one of the men. After she had written her remembrances in detail, she quietly read her notes aloud. She couldn't believe all the details she had forgotten to include. It took nearly twenty additional minutes before she was comfortable with all she had written. A similar scene was taking place in Joyce's bedroom after she had finished her supper.

Neither Joyce nor Amanda could get those two men out of her mind. They were afraid of them but hoped to help make sure they were caught for what they had done. They didn't want anyone in Merrysville to get robbed or killed. They decided they had to talk to their mothers about it. They were sure their mothers would know what to do. Both girls were exhausted and fell into a fitful sleep, with the argument of those two men still going through their minds.

Chapter 7

Murderers Revealed

Joyce called Amanda early the next morning, and asked, "Did you think about those guys all night?" Amanda said, "I did. Before I went to bed, I made many pages of notes of everything I remembered hearing the men say. I could hardly sleep. I didn't tell Mother or Dad yet though. Did you tell your mother?" Joyce admitted that she didn't know what to tell her. Like Amanda, she couldn't tell her mom at breakfast without her brother wondering where she heard such a scary conversation.

Amanda asked, "What should we do Joyce?" Joyce answered, "Please get your mom and come over here. My mother and I are here alone, so it would be a good time for us to discuss our concern about those two men. I know my mother and yours will give us good advice." Amanda turned around and asked her mother, "Would you please come with me to talk to Joyce and her mom?" Betty stood up and followed her young daughter next door, wondering all the way just what kind of a surprise the girls had cooked up this time. As soon as they arrived, Amanda quickly told Joyce, "Those two men from the barn came to our house last night. They lied to Dad by telling him they had just arrived from their homes in Philadelphia."

Remembering the two men she fed the night before; Betty was speechless at the news. Iris Belle came into the room, smiled at Betty, and then noticed that Betty and both girls were very concerned about something. She asked, "Hey! What's up?"

Before Amanda could even think of an answer, Joyce blurted out, "Let me just tell you what we heard yesterday." She told their moms everything the girls had heard in the barn. She explained, "When the men were talking in the barn, they said that one of the men had mugged and might have killed someone in a Chicago suburb, just sixty miles from their homes. Later when they were next door, they told Amanda's dad they were from Philadelphia." She was so nervous recalling the time in the barn when she asked her mother, "Why would they do that, Mother? Why would they lie?"

Her mother smiled and told the girls, "They probably said that as a cover-up. In case anyone in Merrysville heard about the murder, they wouldn't be suspected of committing the crime near Chicago."

Iris Belle told the girls she would tell Joyce's dad as soon as he came home for lunch. A short time later, she sent the girls to the store to buy some lemons. They had hardly gone when the doorbell rang. There stood two men, looking very neat.

The short man told Iris Belle how grateful they were that they had come to Merrysville. They were grateful that the village had nice clean bathrooms with showers for visitors of the village to keep clean. "They're safe because they are right behind your fire station."

The tall man nodded and told her that they had eaten a nice meal next door the previous afternoon. They offered to do any work Iris Belle had if she would provide them with lunch. She suggested that they could split some of the logs at the back of their lot for her fireplace. She said, "After you finish cutting the wood for an hour, you should sit in the backyard at the table with an umbrella on it. The sun gets hot at this time of day. In the meantime, I'll fix something nutritional for you two for your lunch."

Amanda and Joyce came back from the store and Joyce exclaimed, "Mom, those two men in the back yard are the ones we told you about." Iris Belle nodded, "I thought they might be. Stay away from the door so they don't see you. I fixed you girls a tuna salad sandwich and some chips that you can eat while you relax. In the meantime, I'll take some soup, chips, and a large tuna salad on fresh greens from the garden for the men to eat."

When Joyce's dad came into the house, Iris Belle nervously told him the situation. He called his friend, the county sheriff. Her dad described the two men and asked if he had heard anything about a mugging or murder near Chicago.

Chapter 8

An Anonymous Caller

The sheriff confided that his deputy had taken a call from a man the previous day. He said the caller was quite shook up as he explained, "I was lying on a pile of straw on the floor of an empty boxcar of a freight train near Chicago, when I suddenly heard two men yelling and running toward the train. The light was shining on the two men when they jumped into the other end of the boxcar. One man was very tall, and the shorter man was about five foot eight. I could tell they were arguing about a man that one of them had just hurt badly or killed near Chicago." The deputy asked the anonymous caller his name and asked if either man had called the other man by his name.

The caller sounded afraid someone might be listening. "No, no names were mentioned. I never moved, but I pretended to be asleep. It was dark in the boxcar, so I didn't think the men saw me. As the train passed a light, I saw the taller man was fanning several bills. He was bragging because he had gotten several hundred dollars from the injured man's pocket. I heard the other man say, 'I really feel badly that you hurt that man because I only asked him for enough to eat a meal. I expected the man to give us change or a dollar. When he handed me ten dollars, I could not believe our blessing and thanked the man. I was shocked when you told him that was not enough and tried to grab money out of his front pocket. When you told him that you could see that he had a lot of money in that pocket, I could not believe I heard right. I saw him crying when he told you that he had cashed his income tax return check to surprise his wife."

"When I pleaded with you to leave him alone, you acted like you didn't even hear me. You knocked him down and hit his head with that big rock. I feel like you killed him. What has gotten into you? Will you want to kill me next?'"

The deputy could tell the caller was crying, as he continued, "By this time, the shorter man was crying, and the taller man said, 'I don't know why I did something like that. Of course, I would never kill you. I saw a woman as she came out of the restaurant. She saw me hit him, so I grabbed the money and ran.'"

"My deputy had to ask the caller three times if he was still on the line. Finally, he spoke, through sobs, and said, "I think I may have been followed. No, I guess not. Well, the shorter man stopped crying long enough to speak in sobs, 'When you grabbed the money and the woman screamed, a lot of people looked out the window of that restaurant and saw the whole thing."

"I looked up and you were running toward the railroad that we had just left. The woman kept screaming. When I put my jacket under the man's head, I yelled for her to call an ambulance. I didn't have any water, but I put my white handkerchief on the man's head to stop the bleeding. I should have stayed, but I was in shock. I told the man I would pray for him, and I have. When I heard the ambulance coming, I was a coward and started running to follow you. I keep asking myself, 'Why didn't I stay?' The short man stood up, and shook his head back and forth, as if to awaken from a bad dream."

The caller told the deputy, "The short man nearly screamed, 'I feel like I just had a bad nightmare. I still cannot believe that within minutes we have become criminals, fugitives, maybe murderers, just to get the money for one meal. I don't know if anyone saw us catching this moving train or not. In all the years I've known you, I have never known of you hurting anyone. I still can't understand why you did it."

The caller told the deputy that it sounded like the shorter man sat down and was crying at the other end of the car. The other man kept yelling at him to get over it. The caller said the men got off at a place called Merrysville.

The informant was talking quietly as if someone was near him. He nearly whispered, "I have to remain anonymous because the tall man noticed me as they were jumping off the train. In the dark, I don't think he saw what I look like. I sure hope not."

"The shorter man probably saved my life because he told the tall man he was sure the man in the straw was dead. I'm sorry but I can't give your office my name because I don't want to be killed by the two men. If it hadn't been for the short man, that other man would have killed me. I just know he would have." The deputy said there was silence on the line as the man hung up the phone.

The sheriff, Nelson Webb, told Joyce's dad that he had received a notice from a suburb of Chicago describing two men. "They fit the same description as the men that the anonymous caller saw. They are being hunted for robbery and mugging of a man outside a restaurant. The mugged man has been in a coma since then. A woman witnessed all of it. She thought the shorter man was a doctor because he started to help the injured man."

"Other people eating in the restaurant had only seen the outline of two men, one very tall and one medium height. When the ambulance was coming, customers went outside the restaurant but the short man was running away from the scene. They could not describe either man. It sounded like a robbery gone wrong."

The sheriff told Joyce's dad to keep an eye on the men to see where they were going. He and two deputies would be in Merrysville in about twenty minutes to pick them up. Joyce's dad took dishes of ice cream and a plate of cookies out to the men and talked to them about what kind of work they were seeking. They told him they enjoyed working in a factory. He told them that he didn't think there were any openings in factory work anywhere near Merrysville, but he had seen a large "Help Wanted" sign in the front yard of the grain elevator this morning. It was located on the other side of the railroad tracks.

The faces of both men lit up. The shorter man spoke, "That sounds like it could be a permanent job for us. We both like this village and are sure our families would like to get out of Philadelphia because there's no work there." Iris Belle took a glass of fresh lemonade for her husband, and a full pitcher of lemonade with lots of ice. The two men drank another glass of the lemonade, then stood up and said they would go check out the grain-elevator job.

Chapter 9

Arrested

As the two strangers were coming out of the drugstore, they were laughing about something Miss Barnes had told them. The tall man was casually unwrapping a stick of gum he had just purchased. He offered a stick to the other man. As they stuck the gum into their mouths, the sheriff's car pulled up beside them.

A deputy got out on the passenger's side and asked the men to see their driver's licenses. He looked at the licenses. When he saw they were from a city near Chicago, he nodded to the sheriff. The sheriff and the other deputy exited the vehicle and told them, "You are being arrested on Suspicion of Robbery and Attempted Murder. A witness heard you discussing your crime on the train."

It dawned on both men that the man they saw lying on the straw at the opposite end of the empty freight car was neither asleep nor dead when they thought he was. They looked at each other and shook their heads. The tall man screamed, "I told you to let me take care of him." The short man said, "We didn't even see what he looked like."

" I'm thinking of that poor man near Chicago. I should have gone back when I heard the ambulance was coming." The tall man looked at him like he had lost his mind.

The sheriff and one of his deputies handcuffed the men. As he opened the back door of the sheriff's car, the deputy saw the shorter man was shaking and crying. Both men climbed into the back seat. One of the deputies got in the back seat from the other door. Neither suspect said a word.

Everyone watching could hardly believe how easily the sheriff's office did their job. With the crowd that had gathered outside the drugstore, the sheriff was concerned that the town marshal might be nearby.

It soon was all over town that the sheriff had arrested two strangers in Merrysville from a tip from a man on a train. Whew! That made the girls feel much safer. The story going around town was that the tall man gave the deputy all the money he had stolen from a man he mugged.

The news on the radio and in the newspaper described the incident where the man was mugged. The mugging was in front of a restaurant window with several people near the window. The Cook County sheriff knew that only one witness saw the mugger use the rock they found behind the injured man. Finger printers should soon know the identity of the mugger.

The next day, Amanda said, "Joyce, I wonder how those two men are doing. What do you think has happened to them?" Joyce shook her head, "I'm sure, or should say, I doubt that we will ever know. Being this far from Chicago, we probably won't hear anything about it on the radio or read anything about it in the local papers."

Chapter 10

Witness Needed

A few days later, a call came from Sheriff Webb. He told Joyce's dad that the sheriff from Illinois had come to the jail last week and taken the attempted murder suspects back to the Chicago suburb where the crime was committed. All money stolen from the man was returned. The suspects still had a ten-dollar bill that the victim had given them as a gift.

The Cook County sheriff later called the Sheriff Webb's office to notify them that the victim was still unconscious. The doctor told the family he could not say for sure that the man would make it.

The robbers hadn't spent a cent of the stolen money. What a senseless crime. The two men were going to be charged with Robbery and Assault. If the victim died before the trial in six weeks, the suspected men would be charged with Second Degree Murder at the trial.

The Cook County Prosecutor's office wanted help. They needed a witness who heard the men talking about their part in the murder. He knew if such a witness came forward, it would help the trial to go quickly. The Cook County Sheriff questioned the whereabouts of the man who had been on the train with them.

Sheriff Webb reminded him, "The unidentified caller never came into our office. It was apparent that he feared for his life. He left the area before he could be questioned by our sheriff's office. He never filled out any legal paperwork."

Sheriff Webb hesitated, and then told the Illinois caller, "I'm not sure if there's any truth to it. Someone told me, in confidence, that two young girls they know, heard two men arguing. They mentioned a man they had mugged, and maybe killed, outside a bar in a Chicago suburb. They said the girls were only ten years old. If it is true, I doubt if the girls or their parents would be willing for them to testify. Would their identity be told to the public, attorneys, or the men?"

The Cook County Sheriff said, "Because of their age, the girls would give depositions which would be particularly important for the trial that was set for four weeks. Their names would not be exposed." He urged Sheriff Webb to find out the identity of the girls.

The Cook County Sheriff told Sheriff Webb to tell the parents that their daughters should come to Chicago to give a sworn deposition as testimony of what they had heard the men saying to each other. It was the American thing to do.

Sheriff Webb cleared his throat before he continued, "Wait a moment! Personally, I think that is a bit much to expect of any ten-year-old. Just how do you think they would get to Chicago? I'll be honest with you, if they were my daughters, I would never think of letting them testify, let alone come to your city. I doubt if you would either."

"They are too young to subpoena. I will try to find out who they are, but don't count on their cooperation. I don't."

When Sheriff Webb called Joyce's dad, he told him everything he and the other sheriff had discussed. "Since the girls are ten years old, the Cook County sheriff told me that the girls would not have to be in the courtroom. They would give their story, under oath, directly to the sheriff's court officer in the suburb of Chicago where the man was mugged. That is called a deposition. If their depositions sound credible, they will be read in court. Because they are minors, they would not be required to give their testimony in front of the two men. Their names would be known only to the court."

Mr. Perkins told the sheriff he would talk to his wife and the Martins before they decided what to do. He promised to call the sheriff back in a short time to let him know if the girls were interested. The sheriff reminded him, "Remember, the trial is already set for six weeks."

"I am not sure what I would do if I were you or the Martins, but I personally think those two girls would do just great if they would like the adventure. I have great confidence in them." Both men laughed, and Mr. Perkins agreed, "So do I."

Chapter 11

Grown up at Ten

All four parents felt it was too much to ask of their daughters, but the girls thought it sounded exciting. Both girls said they felt they would be safe if they did not have to face the two men, or if the men could not find out who they were or where they lived. That was a relief. They agreed to testify that they were hiding behind bales of straw, about ten feet away from the men, where they were able to hear everything they said. That was the truth. They would not mention that it was the straw in their upstairs hideout. They did not have to mention it was in the barn.

The girls had never told the sheriff nor anyone except Mr. Andy and their mothers about the hideout. It scared the girls when they talked about having to describe where they were when they heard the men talking. They knew they had to tell the truth since they would be under oath, but they did not want to divulge their secret. They were more excited about going to Chicago than they were scared. The sheriff suggested they do it in two weeks. The girls and their parents agreed to that time.

They had two weeks before they had to be there, and both girls were thinking about what they would wear. They did not think they had any suitable clothes to wear to a courthouse, so they discussed talking to their mothers and suggesting that it would be neat if they could get their moms to agree to take them into Chicago a few days before they had to give their testimony. They could shop and perhaps see some of the city. They were so excited about the entire idea they could hardly wait to see what their mothers would say.

When Joyce got home that evening, she found her mother was alone in the kitchen preparing dinner. She told her, "Mom, since we have to go to Chicago to talk about what we heard those men say, Amanda and I were talking about…" Her mom smiled, nodded, and Joyce continued, "what fun it would be if it was just the four of us." Joyce thought about the best way to say what she wanted. "Well Mom, could just you moms and us girls go into Chicago for a few days? No dads, no brothers."

"We could go a few days early and shop one day and see some of the places that you and Dad have talked about being so great in Chicago. You mentioned the planetarium that would be fun to see at night. If we could give our deposition on Monday or Tuesday, it would be great if we went early and stayed in the same room at a hotel. Maybe next month there could be a Dad and Son weekend. What do you think?"

Her mother laughed, "Wow! You two must have been busy talking about this a lot to come up with such a neat idea. I will talk it over with your dad tonight. If he feels that he and your brother can survive that long without us, I will talk to Amanda's mother first thing in the morning."

"You two girls should start writing down everything you remember about the discussion you overheard. You should document the fact that you heard the men arguing about mugging and possibly killing someone in a Chicago suburb, but then Mr. Martin said they told him they were from Philadelphia. If Amanda's parents agree to this plan, we will have to agree to **not** let your brothers know the real reason we're going. Don't forget, the sheriff said that your lives could be in danger if your involvement is ever made public." Joyce agreed.

Both of Amanda's parents agreed with Joyce's parents that it would be a wonderful way to avoid a need to answer any questions about going into Chicago for a day. Amanda's mother, however, insisted that the sheriff not report that the men had mentioned living near Philadelphia. The men would remember to whom they told that story.

Since neither woman wanted to drive in Chicago, Iris Belle suggested it would be fun to take the train. Betty loved that idea and was sure the girls would embrace the opportunity. The plan was to leave on Thursday, in less than two weeks. After they finished their shopping on Thursday afternoon and part of Friday, they would plan to see the Museum of Science and Industry, the Aquarium, and if there was enough time, the Planetarium on Friday or Saturday evening. Joyce's dad suggested, "Why not take a boat ride one evening to see the Chicago skyline? That is one spectacular sight."

The women planned to be watching for a church on Thursday and Friday while they were out shopping. After they attended a service on Sunday morning, they could treat the girls to eat at a fancy restaurant and take in a movie. The more they discussed it, the more exciting it sounded to all four of them.

Most of Mrs. Hall's raspberries had been picked by that time. Both girls talked to their brothers who agreed they would finish picking any late bloomers. Amanda's dad promised to refrigerate the berries until the women and girls returned.

Chapter 12

Chicago, Here We Come

The Saturday before they were to go, Joyce's grandparents came over for dinner. When her grandmother heard them talking about their plans, she said, "I think I'll join you. It sounds like such fun." Her grandfather shook his head, and quickly spoke up, "It sounds like plans have already been made.…just something special for the girls and their moms." Joyce quickly agreed, "Right! No Grandma, not this time. We love you, but this is a mother-daughter mini-vacation."

Her grandmother looked from Joyce, over to Iris Belle, "What do you think? I could buy Joyce some nice clothes for school and church. I would be happy to treat for all the meals. After all, I'm your mother, and you're my daughter."

Iris Belle shook her head, and simply said, "Thanks for the offer, but you heard Joyce, not this time Mother. It's time for Joyce to choose some of her own school clothes."

Joyce was so proud of her mother. What fun she knew she would have, getting to pick out her own clothes for the sixth grade.

Her grandfather smiled and, turning to Joyce, said, "You'll have a ball, Joyce." Obviously disappointed and hurt, her grandmother quickly changed the subject.

The girls continued to visit their hideout nearly every day after they picked berries. The summer was also busy with work, tennis lessons, and practice. They were grateful that the men coming off the train usually stayed in town one day. They knew they already had enough excitement in their lives for now.

Meanwhile, the girls visited the barn a couple of rainy days with their brothers and friends. They played hopscotch each time. They made sure their hopscotch rocks were saved in a drawer of the office. One day, everyone took a brown bag lunch from home to eat while there, with everyone being careful to clean everything before they left.

All their friends wanted to know why they were getting to go into Chicago in the summer just to shop for school clothes. The ten days went by quickly because the girls could also talk to their friends about the fun time they planned to have with their mothers. When they shared all the activities they would do, most friends were envious and vowed to talk their mothers into doing the same thing.

They just had to remember that they could not mention the court hearing to anyone. They knew their friends and brothers would probably blab to someone, and it would be the talk of the town in less than a day.

The plan was for the girls to take only two changes of clothes and leave space in the big suitcases for the clothes that they would choose in Chicago.

When the day finally came for their trip to Chicago, their dads and brothers took them to the train station, and before they knew it, they were in the Chicago Train Station. The size of the Station and trains overwhelmed Joyce. She commented, "Amanda, have you ever seen anything like this?" Amanda was busy staring at everything. Of course, she had to agree, "No Joyce, never!" The sounds of hissing steam and train engines made it hard to hear each other.

The mothers quickly took their daughters inside the building to buy a map of the city. They discovered a small hamburger restaurant nearby where they could sit down. They ate their sandwiches while they studied the map to make their plans. From there they took a taxi, and dropped off their luggage at the downtown hotel, where Iris Belle had made reservations.

The four shoppers visited several small shops that had pre-teen clothes, but they saw nothing they liked. Joyce's face looked a little forlorn as she uttered, "Amanda and I thought that every store in this city would have hundreds of clothes that we would love, but I don't think Chicago has anything we'd choose.

I don't know how Grandma finds such nice clothes for me. Indianapolis is much smaller than Chicago." When Amanda put her arm around Joyce and agreed, her mom spoke up and said, "I think it's time that we visited Marshall Field's." They spent nearly a day there.

The girls had never seen anything like Marshall Field's for shopping. Both girls knew how much money they could spend on clothes. For the first time in her life, Joyce was able to choose clothes she would feel comfortable in and proud to wear. Amanda had never been interested in girls' clothing before but, at Marshall Fields, she found many items that she felt made her look great. She even felt different in the nice clothes that were available to her. Both girls and moms had a ball.

The girls modeled all styles and colors of dresses, skirts, blouses, and sweaters, often smiling and laughing with pleasure. Sometimes the clothes made them frown. Their mothers could hear them asking each other, "How does this one look?" "Great!" "Wow! I think this looks good." "I love this color. What do you think?" "Could I wear this to school?" The women loved to sit and watch the girls as they modeled many outfits before each chose the ones that she felt looked best on her. Both mothers were proud of the choices their daughters made. The girls spent all the money in their budget.

Never have any females had more fun than the two girls had with their moms during their time together. They went everywhere they had planned, as well as seeing the Field and Nature Museum, Art Museum, and the Zoo. They laughed a lot and felt like they really knew each other better. They attended church on Sunday at the Moody Bible Institute on Clark Street. The four of them discussed that service for many months.

On Tuesday morning, the sheriff sent a car to take the four of them for the girls' depositions. The female officer loaded their luggage into the trunk of the official car. She teased them about how heavy the bags were since they had been shopping. Both girls nodded and laughed.

When Betty met the official from the court who recorded the girls' statements, she was reminded of Mrs. Santa Claus. The court official looked so cheerful with her pink round cheeks and smiling blue eyes as she did her job well, making each witness feel comfortable.

The woman complimented them on their clothes, pointing out the good quality of the fabric, and the fact that the color of each blouse made the girl's eyes seem brighter. She kept eye contact with the girls and told them what a great job they did in recalling even small details about the men in the statements. She was amazed at how the girls told the same story, but in their own way. She loved to watch their expressions as they displayed their shock at what they had heard.

The girls had thought they would be in the room together as each gave her testimony, and planned to add to each other's comments, but their statements were taken separately. When each girl had given her deposition, the court employee came into the waiting room and gave both girls a genuine hug.

The driver of the Sheriff's car took the moms and daughters to the Chicago Train Station where they had lunch before catching the train back to Merrysville.

On the train ride home that afternoon, the girls sat, quietly looking out the train window for a few minutes, then Amanda turned around and blurted out, "I'll be honest, I was just scared silly when I had to be the first to give my testimony, witness, or deposition, whatever you want to call it. After all, we thought we would be together and could hear what the other one said. That lady said I did good, but I don't remember a thing I said. I hope it can help them at the trial." Joyce quickly chimed in, "Because I didn't have any idea of what you said, I was scared to death, to say the least. When she looked at me and told me it was very important that I try to remember exactly what I had heard the men say, I tried to remember. I hope it was something like you remembered. That lady was nice to me."

Recalling the woman's personality, Joyce added, "She sounded like she meant it when she said, 'You girls are wearing beautiful clothes.' When I told her that we had picked out our own clothes in Chicago, and that we would be wearing them to church and school, she said she was impressed. She made me feel a little calmer."

"Also, I thought that if our clothes looked good to a woman with an important job like hers, we must have done a good job in our shopping. After all, her clothes were really nice." Both girls looked at each other, nodded, felt giddy, laughing, and talking to their moms and each other at the same time. When they finally started to relax, both girls were sound asleep within minutes.

The girls felt rested when the train stopped in Merrysville. The girls hugged their dads and brothers who were waiting for them at the train station. Amanda sounded like a travel agent when she suggested that John and Jimmy needed to have a mini father and son vacation in Chicago.

Joyce nodded, then told her brother and dad, "I agree. Be sure to take at least four days or you will never get to see what you'll want to see." Joyce laughed, then repeated, "At least four days. There is so much to see in Chicago."

Betty Martin suggested, "You guys should look at our maps and notes. What a vacation you'll have!" Both girls shocked their families when they confirmed Betty's suggestion by a loud, "Wow-e-e-! "

Chapter 13

MISTER X, Y, OR Z

It was a rather cloudy day when two young boys, nearly twelve years old, walked into Merrysville at about 4:30 in the afternoon, in the middle of June. One of them was limping; they looked like they had walked a long way, and they were tired, sweaty, thirsty, and wanted to rest.

The two boys discovered there was a park at the edge of town and headed in that direction. As they looked around, they saw a big barn and decided to check it out. The roosters' ***Cock-a-doodle-doo! Cock-a-doodle-doo!***" nearly scared the wits out of both boys as they passed by the front of the building on their way around to the back.

They noticed signs on the barn doors. The blond boy told his brother, "Look at this funny sign. It says 'Welcome to The Barn That Crows'. I wish they had a sign at the entrance of this park so those roosters wouldn't have scared us so." When they looked over to the park to see what it looked like, they saw several children from the town, playing along the edge of a pond.

They opened the door that invited them to come in. The taller boy pointed to the large sink inside the barn and headed in that direction. There were many tall aluminum glasses on the shelf. The ice-cold water was so inviting that both boys drank quite a bit, then splashed the water all over their faces and hair. They were laughing and yelling at the same time. The two girls in their hideout had not seen the boys as they entered the park. They looked at each other and shrugged their shoulders as they tried to visualize who might be downstairs acting that way over a sink of water.

 ©Annabelle Sandlin

After they left the barn, the boys went to the walkway and watched the local kids for a while. They all looked happy and seemed to be having fun. The two boys decided to go down and see if they were friendly. The girls watched the boys from their window and wondered who they were. When the boys had cleared the barn area, the girls were soon behind them.

Both boys were a sight to behold. Their clothes and hair were dripping wet. The taller boy looked like he had been in a fight or had fallen. His clothes were filthy and dripping mud. The boys walked shyly toward a lone boy who was tinkering with his fishing pole. The blond-haired boy introduced himself to the fisherman. His name was Tom Jackson, and the other boy was his brother Ron. The stranger told them that his name was Bob Perkins.

Ron asked Bob if that was a good fishing pond; it began a conversation about fishing for some time. Bob explained that you had to be a member to fish there. Only residents of the county could be members. When he showed Tom and Ron his day's catch, they were impressed.

Bob finally asked them where they lived. Tom told him they lived in Butler Bluff, not really a village. It wasn't far from Marshall's Corner. Tom pointed north and explained that Marshall's Corner was a very small village in that direction. He sounded exhausted as he explained that he and his brother started to take a small hike early that morning before breakfast and lost their way. That's how they ended up at the park in Merrysville. Bob had never heard of Butler Bluff nor Marshall's Corner.

When Bob asked, "Ron, why are you limping?" Before Ron could say a word, Tom explained, "Ron tripped over a log when he heard a strange noise and turned to look another way. His leg was bleeding, but the blood has dried." Bob felt bad for the two boys but couldn't see what the solution was to their being lost. He looked at the boys, "I'm sorry you're lost. What are you going to do? Where are you going from here? It's almost evening."

They looked like they were going to cry; they shook their heads and admitted they didn't know what to do, or where to go. They had never been to Merrysville so they didn't know how to go home. The girls started to join the group to get acquainted but stopped when they saw Bob's five friends going over to meet the new boys. Bob introduced them and explained their predicament. Amanda and Joyce saw that Bob had everything under control, so the girls headed home.

Bob sized up the situation, and asked, "You must be starved if you missed breakfast. If you don't have a plan yet, would you like to go home with me until you decide what you are going to do? My family might have a solution if you need a ride home." The boys looked at each other. Bob continued, "My mom will give you something to eat. Maybe you will be able to think better on a full stomach." "She's a great cook," was confirmed by Bob's friends.

Both boys looked relieved and were even able to smile at the thought. Bob and Jimmy put their arms around the boys' shoulders as the seven boys proceeded toward Bob's house. One by one, the other boys stopped at their house along the way.

Joyce waved goodbye to Amanda and went into the house as the kids came down the driveway. When they reached Bob's house, his father drove onto the driveway. He smiled and asked, "Who are these two boys? I don't think we've met before." Bob said they were his new friends Ron and Tom Jackson. He let his dad know that he and his friends had just met them at the park today.

Tom spoke up and smiled when he told Bob's dad, "We're twins, but no one has ever guessed it because we don't look that much alike. Ron has dark hair, and he's a little taller than I am." Tom was blond and had handsome dimples when he smiled. Both had blue eyes and fair complexions. Tom was right. They didn't look like twins. But then, neither did Bob and Joyce.

After the boys met Joyce Perkins, they looked up at her brother Bob and his dad before Bob spoke to Ron and Tom. "Come on into our house. We can clean up that leg, and our mom will know what to put on it to keep it from getting infected. It doesn't look good, does it, Dad?"

His dad agreed that it needed attention, and added, "You boys look like you've been gone for a long time. You should call your mom and dad so that they won't be worried about you." The boys nodded in agreement. Everyone heard Tom's stomach as it began growling quite loudly. He blushed as he admitted, "We haven't had anything to eat since seven o'clock last night." Everyone went into the house so the boys could meet Iris Belle. Art introduced them and let Iris Belle know the boys hadn't eaten for over twenty-two hours.

Iris Belle was wearing a blue dress, with a lovely white half apron tied around her waist. The apron had a lovely blue pocket made from the dress material. Ron smiled and told Iris Belle, "You look beautiful in that dress. Our mother has a beautiful blue dress just like yours. Doesn't she Tom?" Tom smiled and nodded, "Your dress is just like Mother's, but she doesn't have that pretty apron to go with it." Bob was quick to tell the boys that his mother made her dress and all the beautiful aprons that she wore. Tom was surprised but said his mother had made her dress as well.

As soon as she saw the dried blood, Iris Belle, began cleaning and treating the wound. While she was helping Ron, both boys were talking as fast as they could to tell her everything that her husband and children had just heard. She suddenly remembered that Art told her that the boys hadn't eaten since seven o'clock last night and were really hungry. Fortunately, Iris Belle had made her famous bean soup and cornbread that afternoon. She went to the refrigerator and produced a large plate of left-over meatloaf and home-made bread for sandwiches. What a feast they shared.

Before the boys called their mother, they explained that they had no idea where their dad was. Their parents, Elmer and Sarah Jackson, owned the joint grocery store/restaurant and post office at Butler Bluff. Most of their customers were farmers and people from other small villages who worked in the cities. They also had two gas pumps and free tire air. Fourteen months ago, their dad took off a broken part of one of the gas pumps. He planned to take it to South Bend for a replacement part. Ron told them that they only had one gas pump since their dad left. Nobody knew how to repair the pump without the missing part.

Their mother had only received one phone call from their dad. The call was received when their dad was less than an hour from home. He let their mother know that he had a flat tire on their old truck. He had described the gas station he was calling from and the highways that intersected in front of it. When the tire went flat while he was driving, he knew the tire had picked up a nail because the tires were relatively new. He said it was raining cats and dogs, and he could hardly see to drive into the service station. The station was fixing the flat while Elmer had a Coke and called home.

Their dad planned to proceed when the rain slowed down. It started pouring a few minutes after he left and hadn't let up. It rained hard off and on all that day. When their dad didn't return home that night, Sarah contacted the State Police, with a description of his truck and license number. No one had heard from him nor seen his truck in fourteen months. Both boys started to cry. Iris Belle gave Ron and Tom hugs and a napkin. When they stopped crying, she took them into her office so they could talk to their mother.

Sarah Jackson cried from relief when she heard Tom's voice. She had called the police and reported her sons missing at two p.m. Iris Belle talked to their mother to get the directions for driving them home. Sarah said she would call the State Police to report that her sons had gotten lost and were safe.

Joyce had run next door to tell Amanda about the sad situation and they agreed that they had to solve that mystery for the Jackson family.

Everyone piled in the big old Buick and sang as they returned their new friends to their mother. She invited them in for apple cider and donuts. Their mom was beautiful and looked too young to have a fourteen-year-old daughter and twelve-year-old twin boys. Yvonne, the daughter said she and the boys were the attendants at the gas pumps during the summer and evenings.

The Jackson family had one full-time and one part-time employee. The employees helped Sarah to cook and wait on tables. Everyone helped people coming to get their groceries, but only Sarah was able to handle the mail.

Her husband, Elmer, was a good mechanic, so he had always been busy taking care of customers' cars. Yvonne was glad to see that her brothers were okay. She said she and her mother were worried when they didn't come home for lunch. Because of their dad being missing, her mother had cried most of the afternoon.

Sarah Jackson said she had talked to all the State Police posts on the road to South Bend after her husband disappeared. Police checked every truck between the miles where Elmer disappeared and South Bend, but no one reported seeing him or his truck. She said she had called all State Police posts once a week for these fourteen months.

Joyce told Mrs. Jackson that she and her friend Amanda loved to solve crimes and planned to help her find her husband. Mrs. Jackson had to smile. She didn't think that two young girls could find Elmer if the state police were unable. She smiled and told Joyce that her family would be grateful if they could.

Joyce asked Mrs. Jackson for a picture or two of her missing husband. She told Mrs. Jackson that she and Amanda always prayed that God would give them wisdom and discernment to find the solutions to problems they helped solve. Her brother Bob looked at Joyce like he thought she was a little kooky. After all, Bob had no idea of anything that she and Amanda had done. On the way home, Joyce was praying silently that God would help Amanda and her to find this man.

Two days later, the girls were in their hideout when the train stopped for water. A short time later, two men entered the barn and were talking about their time in Michigan last month. They talked for quite a while about the tour they were able to take of the Kellogg plant in Battle Creek.

One of the men sounded concerned when he mentioned that nice looking man, they had met the next day when they stopped for coffee in a small town in Michigan. The guy had introduced himself to them as Mr. X. The man from the train wondered why the man had no idea who he was. The man told them that he didn't know when he lost his memory, or where. Both girls smiled and started thanking God for sending these men when the girls were in the barn.

The men left the barn to see if they could get a meal. Both girls felt certain that God had sent those two men to help locate Elmer Jackson, the father of Ron and Tom. They needed to talk to those men alone, so they left their hideout to find them. The girls saw them as they were talking to Amanda's mother and asking for food.

When the men were eating, the girls shared the conversation with Betty. She had the girls take large glasses of lemonade outdoors for the men. The girls told the men, "Friends of ours don't know where their dad is. He disappeared last year. Since he was such a good dad and husband, they know he wouldn't just leave them if he is able to return home. In your travels, in the last fourteen months, have you men ever seen anyone who had lost his or her memory?"

The men looked at each other in surprise. They seemed pleased for the opportunity to talk to someone about the man they met in a restaurant near Baxter, a small town in Michigan, near Battle Creek. One of the men told the girls, "It was only two weeks ago when we were having coffee. We asked the man sitting at the next table how long he had lived there. He told us he couldn't remember where he was from, when he came there, or even his name. He said everyone where he worked called him Mr. "X"."

Both girls were surprised by his answer. Amanda asked what the man looked like. They described him as a clean cut, very good-looking man about 35, about five feet, ten inches tall, with a dark tan, and looked like a body builder. Joyce ran home and brought a picture of Mr. Jackson.

The girls were pleased when the men nodded after they saw the picture. The men couldn't be sure if the man in the wedding picture, taken sixteen years before, was the man they had coffee with, but they thought the picture looked very much like him. The man they saw had a deep tan. The men were sorry that they had no idea where the man was living. When he talked about the men where he worked calling him "Mr. X", he let the men know he had a job, but he never told them what kind of a job he had. The men thought he might be a construction worker or a roofer because of his dark tan.

Both girls were confident that they had enough information to easily find Mr. Jackson. They shared these facts with their families and the sheriff.

The sheriff called the police in Battle Creek and a constable near Baxter. They never heard of a man around their community who didn't know who he was. They felt he must have been a person who was just passing through or someone surely would have called the police if they met him. The sheriff called Amanda and told her the bad news. He encouraged her to call him if she had any more clues.

Just after Amanda hung up, her dad told Betty and the kids that he was going to pick up something he needed for the gardens. The supplier was located at the crossroads where Mr. Jackson disappeared. Amanda asked if she and Joyce could ride along. Her dad agreed that the girls might find out something helpful in the area. Joyce was thrilled to go along. Both girls were silently praying that God would show them where they could find a clue about Mr. Jackson's disappearance.

When Mr. Martin was inside the store, the girls saw an area just about a hundred feet from the store that looked like there had been an accident there in the past. There were permanent deep scars on the road that went all the way to the ditch. They crossed the street and looked down off the highway. Amanda said, "Look Joyce, that ditch is really a bad gully. There's been a lot of water washing it deeper."

It was evident from deep grooves cut through roots and rocks that a vehicle of some kind had gone off the road there and been pulled out by a truck. Dried and deep tracks were in deep sand. Suddenly, Joyce yelled,

"Amanda, look down here. I think I see a license plate." Sure enough, there was about a third of a license plate sticking through the dirt. Joyce kicked it twice, but it didn't budge. She had a hard time wiggling the filthy license plate so it was loose enough to raise it out of the hard dirt. Her hands kept slipping off the thin metal. Amanda was afraid that Joyce was going to get her hands cut so she gave her the nice hanky she had in her pocket. Finally, Joyce raised it in triumph and both girls cheered.

Amanda was looking around for more clues in the bushes, short shrubbery, and green brush nearby. It was evident that one of the bushes had lost two large branches in the past. "Look up, Joyce," she yelled. "I see a ripped green jean jacket in that shrubbery behind you. It blends right in with the bush. No wonder it was never noticed by someone passing in a car. Can you reach it?"

Joyce stood on her toes, but she wasn't quite tall enough. Amanda jumped down near the shrubbery and reached for the jacket. It ripped further as she pulled the stiff, muddy, jacket from the ragged branches.

Amanda squealed, "Joyce, it's heavy. Not just the mud. There must be something in the pockets." By that time, both girls had dried mud on their clothes and faces. Their shoes were filthy. The girls looked all around and walked several feet in each direction but found nothing more. Their hands were scratched as they climbed out of the ditch. They were crying from joy as they carried their new-found treasures to the car. By that time, Mr. Martin was coming out of the store and was concerned when he saw both girls were dirty and crying.

When he saw the items, the girls were holding in their muddy hands, he was amazed. He quickly looked in the pocket of the dirty jacket and found a wallet that had a zipper all around it. The zipper still worked. A small edge of some pictures inside were dirty, but Mr. Jackson's driver's license was still in perfect condition. John started to hug the girls and was crying harder than they were. The other pocket was torn but contained the part that needed to be replaced for the gas pump. Amanda said, "No wonder that jacket was so heavy."

John took the girls inside the gas station and explained about Mr. Jackson's disappearance and apparent accident. One man who appeared to be the owner of the shop remembered the terrible rainy night last year when the man had them remove the nail and put a patch on his tire.

He said, "I remember the incident because the tires were nearly new and still had most of the tread on them. After the man paid for his repair, he jumped into the old truck and said he was headed north."

"He was hardly out of the driveway when the skies opened into a torrential rain. Immediately there was a horrendous noise. A customer thought it was just the loud thunder that came with lightning all around the station. The rain prevented anyone from checking out the noisy accident. We couldn't even see our gas pumps because of the downpour."

"A man who was drenched to the skin came in and said a huge truck from a gravel pit in Michigan had slid on the muddy highway. That truck hit a small truck and pushed it into the ditch. He thought the same big truck pulled the smaller one out of the ditch and took it somewhere."

"The next day the rain had stopped but the road was full of mud One of my employees told me that several cars and trucks had accidents after I went home because of the mud. I never heard anything about individual accidents the previous night."

Mr. Martin asked the station owner if there was a junkyard for cars near the station. The owner pointed north and told him, "Oh yes, there is a large junkyard on the highway going north. It must be at least three miles north, on the right side of the road. The owner of that junkyard has a reputation of having a great memory. If he saw a wreck, he will be able to help you. I'm sorry I can't tell you anything more." The station phone rang as Mr. Martin was thanking him, and the owner excused himself.

Chapter 14

The Hunt is On

Amanda asked her dad, "Dad, could we go there, please? I just have a feeling that God will have the people there remember something that will help us find Mr. Jackson." Joyce nodded and said, "Please Mr. Martin. I feel the same way." John nodded and hugged both girls. He was as interested as the girls to help solve this fourteen-month mystery, so he drove to the junk yard. He had planned to as soon as the service station owner told them about the owner's memory.

The junk yard owner was very friendly and listened intently as Mr. Martin shared the story of Mr. Jackson's disappearance. The man laughed and said, "I know this isn't a laughing matter, but I do remember the truck you're talking about. It was such a wreck that I couldn't even tell you what kind of a truck it was. I don't know how the driver survived. A huge truck from a gravel pit near someplace called Baxter, Michigan brought in that rusty and severely damaged old truck they had hit when they slid across the highway on half a foot of mud, several miles back."

"The truck could never have been repaired. The man driving the big truck asked me if we would be willing to buy the wreck. It just so happened that we were filling an enormous semi load of crushed cars and trucks to send to the Ford plant in Chicago. Their facility melted the cars to make steel and used it for the Army tanks to go overseas. You have to remember that the war was still going on when they were here with the truck to sell."

"I asked the owner of the truck if he wanted to sell it. He was still a little dazed from the accident, but said he needed to get rid of it since it could never be driven. I gave him twenty-five dollars for the truck; I also gave him sixteen dollars, four dollars a tire, since all four were in excellent condition and would sell quickly. I hadn't seen good tires like those for a long time. The war was using available rubber to manufacture tanks and Jeeps."

"The owner and two men from the truck watched while I had the truck crushed and put on the semi that would be going to Ford in Chicago. The men were fascinated as they watched the procedure. The man who had owned the wreck took the forty-one dollars and got into the truck. That was the last time I saw the men."

"I'd never heard of Baxter, Michigan, but if I was hunting for one of my men, I'd go up there and find the gravel pit. Someone there probably remembers him and where he went." Mr. Martin agreed with the man and drove home. All the way home, discussion followed about what they had heard. The three were praising God that He had helped them to learn more than the police had.

When they arrived home, Betty called Iris Belle. The two families discussed what the best plan would be to pursue this further. They didn't want to get Mrs. Jackson's hopes up if she couldn't check it out. Mr. Martin called Information for Baxter, Michigan. There was no separate listing for a Baxter, Michigan. When he called Information for Battle Creek, the reply was, "I'm sorry but I'm not showing a listing for a Baxter Gravel Pit in Baxter or Battle Creek. On the highway, a few miles before you get to Battle Creek, you'll see a couple of houses and a gas station with a street sign in front that identifies it as Village of Baxter, and six or seven more houses. Perhaps you could ask a gas station attendant where it is. In a small burg like that, everyone probably would know." John agreed that was their best plan.

They voted against getting the sheriff or police involved. They knew Mrs. Jackson would still be wondering if her husband was even alive while the police tried to find him. Mr. Perkins had a busy schedule for the entire week, but Mr. Martin had no commitments planned for the next three days. The adults felt it would be best if Mr. Martin took the long company station wagon and drove to Baxter, Michigan.

He, Amanda, and Joyce could pick up the Jackson family in the morning and head north on the highway pointed out by the junkyard manager. Betty would stay behind with Jimmy and answer the company phones. John would call home every other hour and keep Betty informed. She, in turn, would call Iris Belle.

The plan was for Betty to call Sarah Jackson immediately and let her know what the girls had discovered about her husband's disappearance. Betty told Sarah that John and the children were going to go up to Baxter, MI to look for her husband the next day.

She invited Sarah and her family to go with them. Since it was nearly seven p.m., everyone could get a good night's sleep, then John would pick up the Jackson family around seven a.m. Of course, Mrs. Jackson was elated and kept shouting, "Kids! We're going to find your dad tomorrow!" In the background, on the other end of the line, Betty could hear crying and much excitement from the children hoping to see their dad.

The next morning when the station wagon pulled up to the grocery store/gas station/restaurant/post office, the Jackson family was outside waiting. An older gentleman, introduced as a neighbor who had volunteered to run the station and post office, was as excited as the family at the prospect of finding Mr. Jackson. He told them that his wife and daughter were inside helping the cook and waitress run the restaurant. Inside the well-lit restaurant, several people were talking and eating their breakfast.

As soon as the station wagon pulled out of the driveway, Amanda handed the torn jacket and license plate to Mrs. Jackson. Betty had washed and repaired the jacket while the girls washed off the wallet and license plate. Tears filled Mrs. Jackson's eyes as she held the treasures close to her heart. She pulled the wallet out of the jacket pocket and opened it. She found it to be amazing that the zipper had kept the pictures and driver's license dry. She was happy to see that Elmer's money was still inside.

On the three-hour drive, Mr. Martin told the anxious family about how the girls had discovered the whereabouts of their dad. They were all crying and thanking the girls for caring and the prayers they asked. Amanda told Ron, "Ron, there's a verse in the Bible that lets us know that even when you hurt your foot, there was a reason. If you hadn't hurt your foot, you would not have come to Joyce's house and let us know about your dad being missing. Joyce and I wouldn't have prayed that God would help us to find him for you."

Joyce interrupted her and quoted, "Ron, that verse Amanda is telling you about is Romans 8:28 in the New Testament. It says, 'And we know that in all things God works for the good of those who love Him, who have been called according to His purpose.' Amanda and I love Him and know He will help us when we ask."

Ron thanked the girl for helping them. Joyce said to everyone, "We need to pray that God will show us where the gravel pit is and that there is someone there that will be able to tell us where your dad is now."

Sarah Jackson and John Martin were talking in the front seats while the kids were in the two back seats. While the adults talked, the kids got to know each other and played all kinds of games. The girls learned that Yvonne and her twin brothers Ron and Tom had to ride on a school bus nearly an hour in each direction. Their school was in a small town near Lafayette.

When the station wagon pulled into the driveway of the gas station in the small village of Baxter, John Martin talked to the attendant who was filling the gas tank. The man gave Mr. Martin easy directions to the gravel pit, less than three miles out of town.

The gravel pit was huge. Only a small sign, about two feet high, instructed truck drivers where to find the office. When the Martin station wagon emptied out near the large office, a loud siren alerted workers of the gravel pit that it was break time. Many hot and sweaty men passed the station wagon to go inside to cool off and get something to eat and drink. The gravel pit furnished water, soda pop and juice, as well as all kinds of free desserts housed in a refrigerated cabinet behind the receptionist.

The office was noisy. When Mrs. Jackson started to ask the man behind the desk if he knew her husband, someone yelled, "Mr. X, you'd better hurry or you're not going to get any of the dessert."

To his family's amazement, Mr. X walked into the door and the boys ran up to him, "Dad, Dad!" and started to cry. Elmer, no longer Mr. X, was surprised, and his mouth flew open when he recognized his family immediately. For the first time in fourteen months, his memory was returning.

He grabbed the boys up into his tanned arms. Yvonne and Sarah stood watching, then joined their family in a circle hug. There was a lot of crying and hugging. The other workers were amazed that Mr. X now had an identification. They also were amazed that his wife was so beautiful.

The man behind the desk turned to Elmer Jackson and his family. He invited everyone to help themselves to the drinks and goodies. The kids didn't have to be asked a second time. Elmer and Sarah were so delighted to see each other that they could hardly talk. Many eyes in that room were full of tears.

John, Amanda, and Joyce wanted to yell for joy, but stood speechless as everyone in the room were telling Elmer how happy they were for him and his lovely family.

Sarah Jackson gave the office girl Elmer's phone number and driver's license so she had his identity information and home address. The employee returned the license to Elmer, along with his final paycheck. Sarah smiled as she handed him his missing wallet. Within a few minutes, the large station wagon was full again. Sarah sat in the middle of the front seat and surprised Elmer when she handed him the clean repaired jacket that was lost for fourteen months. Elmer's eyes teared as he looked at it in disbelief.

He quickly gave John Martin directions on where to go so he could pick up his belongings. His family went inside his room with him to help carry everything. As they traveled home, the family got reacquainted. Yvonne told her dad about all the times her mother had called the State Police. Elmer's family told him that Mr. Martin and the girls were the ones who learned about what happened after he decided to drive north when it was raining buckets.

John explained that the sheriff and police couldn't find out anything about him because his truck was removed from the scene of the accident immediately. Fourteen months later Joyce found his license plate stuck in the mud. Amanda spotted his jacket tangled in a bush. Fortunately, a witness saw the gravel pit truck slide in the mud, hitting and destroying his truck. All Elmer could say was, "Thank God for Joyce and Amanda looking to help my family find me." Tears followed.

Elmer learned that the large truck drove him and pulled his truck to a junk yard. John told him, "The man at the junk yard bought your truck and paid extra for your tires. The owner of the junkyard invited you three men to watch the old truck being flattened once it was bought by the junk yard."

"Elmer, that man heard you tell the driver of the huge gravel pit truck that you were going north. The owner of the junk yard said you climbed into the back seat and fell asleep as the truck pulled out of his lot." Elmer shook his head and said that he couldn't remember any of those details.

Amanda said, "The men must have figured you were going north to look for work, so they probably took you to the gravel pit where you were hired on the spot. You had forty-one dollars in your pocket, so you could eat and find a room until your payday." Elmer shook his head because he couldn't remember. He thanked Amanda and agreed that she probably had that figured right. He told them that his boss gave him the temporary name of Larry Smith, but the workers all called him Mr. X.

Elmer said he told his landlord his name was Larry Smith, so he was never reported as missing, and the police never knew. Since his license plate was never seen on the highways, nobody was able to report locating him. He said he called the local police after a week or so to see if anyone had reported him missing. Thinking his name was Larry Smith, they told him no.

Elmer was pleased to show his wife the saving account book so she saw he had saved a nice amount of money. The gravel pit work was hard, but the pay was above average. They stopped at a restaurant where John Martin called Betty to tell her the great news that Elmer was found, safe and healthy. After they ate lunch, they headed home. Elmer laughed when his wife showed him the part for the gas pump, still in the repaired pocket of his jacket. As soon as he saw it, he remembered that he was on his way to purchase it. He didn't remember anything about the trip or the accident. Mrs. Jackson let Elmer know the pump couldn't be fixed since the part was missing.

As they neared South Bend, Elmer asked Mr. Martin to please stop at the shop where he was headed fourteen months ago. Everyone found it amusing the way he said it, and they all laughed. He went into the shop and picked up the needed part. One of the employees remembered the phone calls they had received several months ago from Mrs. Jackson and the police asking if he had been there.

What a difference there was on the way home. No more concerns or worry. Happiness, smiles, and joy filled the long station wagon.

The older gentleman was outside on a bench when they pulled into the restaurant/gas station/post office. It looked like several people were inside the restaurant eating supper. Mr. Jackson jumped out of the station wagon, gave their older friend a hug, and proclaimed, "There's no place like home." He hugged John for driving the girls and his family to find him.

Everyone got out of the station wagon and helped empty Elmer's belongings. His wife came around, thanked John, and hugged Joyce and Amanda. She told them that her family would be at their church on Sunday, then followed her family inside.

When the station wagon pulled onto the Martin driveway, the girls ran inside and called the sheriff. They told him everything that happened in the past four days. They sounded serious when they told him that he could have Mr. Jackson removed from his Missing Persons List.

Chapter 15

Sudden Fame

The next thing the sheriff did was to call the local newspaper and told them the heart-warming story. He also called the radio stations. It wasn't even dark before cars from four newspapers and three radio stations pulled into the Martin driveway. The local newspaper called the newspapers in other cities to share this unusual news story. The Perkins family was called over to the Martin home. Both families were interviewed. The boys told how they had met the Jackson boys at the park and brought them to the Perkins house to eat and get a ride home.

The media heard how Joyce had gone down into the ditch when she spotted the license plate nearly buried. Amanda's description of Joyce down in that gully, kicking up dirt and tugging to claim that license plate allowed everyone a good laugh.

Joyce waited a minute and got another laugh from everyone when she described Amanda leaning over and handing her a lovely, dainty lace hanky that she used to finally get the license plate out of the hard dirt. Joyce also shared how Amanda had to climb into the gulley to retrieve the jacket from a high broken bush.

For the next several days, the "Mr. X story" was not only talked about in all houses for miles around, but the story was picked up by Walter Winchell on the evening news. He told how two ten-year old girls did in four days what neither the sheriff nor the State Police was able to do in fourteen months. Arthur Godfrey called and talked to the girls. He invited them to come to his news show but the family didn't have time to go to New York for a five or ten-minute live interview. He played the recording of their conversation on national radio.

Their grandparents and friends from all over the country called to congratulate the two families for helping solve the mystery of a missing dad.

When the girls told the story about everything that happened, they gave God, the boys, and Mr. Martin thanks for it all. Both girls feared that every kid and teacher would know about this when they returned to school that Fall. The girls were embarrassed by their fame and hoped that by September, everyone would have forgotten the publicity. The sheriff told both girls that he and his deputies weren't a bit surprised that they quickly cracked the case. That comment gave both girls the warm fuzzies.

On the following Sunday, the First Baptist pastor let the Jackson family use the entire message time to share how God worked through two ten-year-old Christian girls. The entire Jackson family joined the church that Sunday.

Chapter 16

Grandparents are a Blessing

Jimmy and Amanda's maternal grandparents lived just six blocks from their family and attended the same church. They visited every Sunday after church for dinner. Amanda and Jimmy liked to visit their grandma and grandpa often during the week. Their grandma was teaching both kids how to cook and bake. It was a surprise they didn't want to share with their parents until the right time.

Last week when Amanda went to her grandparents' house, her grandma greeted her with, "Amanda, today you get to climb up my trusty ladder and pick cherries so we can bake some pies." Amanda didn't have the courage to tell her grandma that she was frightened of heights. By the time Jimmy arrived, Amanda had picked a large bucket of sour cherries, and was down off the ladder.

Her grandma used the cherries to teach Amanda and Jimmy how to bake a cherry pie. There were more than enough cherries for three pies. Their grandmother said each of them would make one pie. She then showed them how to safely take the pits out of the cherries.

It was obvious that the kids were competitive when they raced to get their half of the pits removed. At first their grandmother had to tell them to slow down and not take most of the cherry with the pit.

Their grandmother said each of them could sit down and have a small dish of the extra cherries. Each one of them placed the sour cherries into a small dish. The sugar bowl was in front of Jimmy. Jimmy stirred a teaspoon of sugar into his dish and took a big bite. Jimmy could hardly talk after he took one bite. The shocked look on his face confirmed that sour cherries require a lot of sugar. They all laughed about the look on Jimmy's face after that first bite. His lips and tongue were numb for hours.

Their grandmother showed them how much sugar it took for three cherry pies. Wow! No wonder Jimmy was speechless after eating cherries with just one teaspoon of sugar. Next, they learned to grease the pie plates before making a good dough, using just the right amount of flour.

They learned there is a right way to put the bottom dough into the pie plates. After it was greased, they sprinkled just a little flour. After the bottom piecrust was in the pie plate, each of them spooned in many sweetened cherries.

Their grandmother was so much fun. She made a contest to see which of them could put the top piecrust on and crimp the sides perfectly before they trimmed off the remaining crust. "You won Grandma. You won!" Both kids could see that their grandmother's years of experience easily won the contest for her.

The remaining piecrust was rolled out by their grandma. She spread butter over all of it, then put lots of sugar and cinnamon on top. She cut it into squares with a scoop of the sweetened cherries on each square and baked it. The kids stacked the baked tarts on a dish as their grandma filled bowls with the lunch she had just cooked. While the pies were baking, Jimmy and Amanda ate lunch with their grandma and grandpa. The piecrust squares were delicious and soon eaten.

That afternoon, after the pies cooled, they drove the kids home with a cherry pie on each lap. Grandma and Grandpa were having the other cherry pie for their dinner.

Friends of the kids who were headed home after they had worked in the gardens, saw Jimmy and Amanda proudly riding in the rumble seat of their grandparents' car. Everyone waved and secretly wished they could ride there sometime. No one saw their delicious looking golden-brown cherry pies - one that the family ate with supper. The other pie would be welcome tomorrow for dessert. Their parents were glad that they shared their secret with them. Yum, yum, cherry pie.

Grandpa and Grandma had a 1935 Chevrolet, with a rumble seat. The 1935 Chevrolet with the rumble seat was the envy of everyone in Merrysville. It was in excellent condition. The kids sometimes got to help Grandpa wash and wax the car. The back opened, with a seat for the grandchildren to go with them when they shopped in Fort Wayne, the nearest large city, eighteen miles from home. Amanda and Joyce were invited to go one week and on alternate weeks, Jimmy was invited to bring one of his friends.

When Bob was available, he usually had the privilege of riding in the rumble seat when it was Jimmy's turn. All of Joyce and Jimmy's friends offered to ride with them. Everyone loved waving at people from the rumble seat, except for the two times Joyce and Amanda got drenched when it started pouring down rain while they were halfway home from the city.

Chapter 17

Memories on Troop Train

The girls, two of their friends, their brothers, and three of their friends were headed for the barn to play shuffleboard when the train whistle blew at the first crossing. All nine kids turned toward the tracks and waved at the engineer in the window of the locomotive. It was such a noisy train, and it quickly passed.

All the boys and girls covered their faces with their hands while the black soot from the train was flying through the morning air. It was landing on the pavement and grass, as well as in the girls' hair. Every girl leaned over and shook their head to get the soot flying out. It was quite an unusual sight.

Bob suddenly remembered a funny story his mother and Aunt Josephine laughed about every time the family got together. He turned to Joyce and asked her to share about her first experience on a troop train. Her face turned red as a beet. She shook her head no, but all the kids urged her to tell them. She finally shrugged her shoulders and said, "Oh, all right if you really want me to." Everyone nodded.

They sat in a circle, on the grass, to listen to Joyce. She laughed nervously and told the following:

"When Bob and I were four or five, according to the news on the radio, there was unrest throughout the world. The whole world, including the United States, was concerned about their country getting involved if a bad war started soon."

©Annabelle Sandlin

"Most Americans were reminded of World War One that started in 1914 and didn't end until November of 1918."

"Our parents, and all of yours, can remember that the United States was attacked at Pearl Harbor in Hawaii December 7th in 1941, thus bringing the United States into World War Two. All of us probably remember how sad our parents were when it was announced on the radio. Our history class talked about World War One and World War Two just a few weeks before school was out." All the kids nodded and shouted, "Oh, yes!"

Every country was trying to maintain a military force in case their country was attacked.

"Well, so much for my history lesson." The kids all laughed. "It was just a few months before the war started when Mother decided to take me to Ohio to visit Aunt Josephine. Neither Aunt Josephine and Uncle Bob, nor our family had much money."

"Before we left, Mother promised that we would go to the park every day. Her description of the swings, slides and exercise bars sounded like fun. She told me we wouldn't have any money to go anywhere that costs when we were at Aunt Josephine's."

"I was told not to ask for anything to eat or drink when we were away from the house. Aunt Josephine and Uncle Bob were newly married, after he graduated from Purdue University. He had just started his new job in Ohio, and Mother knew they didn't have any extra money either."

"Dad and Bob drove us to the Merrysville Depot during the night. When we were waiting for the train to come, Bob and I went outside of the building and listened to the frogs who were croaking over at the park Boy, were they noisy! We also heard crickets all around us, chirping loudly. Lightning bugs were by the ponds, but not near us. Mother and I boarded the train at about one a.m. I blew Dad and Bob two or three kisses through the window from my seat."

"Dad drove Bob home after we waved at them when the train blew its whistle and pulled away from the railroad station."

"I immediately learned why this was called a Troop Train. The train was full of young men wearing U.S. Army uniforms. They told Mother and me they were being shipped to a base where they might be sent overseas if they were needed. Most of them were awake and talking to each other about where the Army would station them."

"Mother mentioned how unhappy they all looked. She told me they reminded her that her brother, my uncle, was already overseas. I had no idea where overseas was. Before Mother closed her eyes, she told me to try to sleep."

"When I looked at the men closely, I knew that Mother was right. Some were nervous and some claimed they were looking forward to defending the USA. I saw how unhappy they all looked so I slid off my seat and walked up to the seat across the aisle. The soldiers smiled when I told them my name was Joyce, and I hoped that I could attend kindergarten that fall. I started telling them stories about my playhouse, our dog, my dad, and twin brother."

"I stayed awake for the entire six hours, entertaining the troops in my special way. I told them that my uncle was in the Army and had visited our family for Christmas. When I told them that my mother had been crying when she thought about her brother being overseas, some of the men cried. By that time, soldiers from many seats were standing around listening to me."

"When I told them that we were going to my aunt's and that my mother told me that we could go to the park for fun since Aunt Josephine was like us, she didn't have any money either. I smiled and told them that I liked going to the park so I could swing high and go down the slide. The soldiers started taking dollar bills out of their wallets and told me that I should treat my mother, aunt, and uncle to eat out or go to a movie when we got there. There was so much money that I had to unzip Mother's purse, put the money in, and close the zipper."

"I thanked the nice soldiers and told them that we sure would have a good time, thanks to them. After I told them that my brother taught me how to do flip flops, I showed them how good I had learned. The men cleared the aisle for me and clapped when I took a bow."

"I told them about going to church and learning that God loved everybody and that Jesus died for all of us. I told them that every week our Sunday School class prays for everyone who is in our military. They were happy to hear that my mother, dad, brother, and I prayed for them at every meal and at bedtime. I told them that even if they were being shot at, they needed to remember God was with them. I told them about some of the times God had taken care of me and my friends."

"I had them laughing and no longer looking like they wanted to cry. That pleased me so much that I asked if I could kiss each of them on the cheek. Everyone said I could. When some cried, I put my hand on their cheek and told them I was so sorry that I made them cry. They smiled and told me that, with my blond ringlets and blue eyes, I reminded them of a younger sister or neighbor."

"One man who said his name was Tom Timmons, told all of us that his mother, dad, and beautiful little six-year-old sister, had been killed in a car accident just a few months ago. The next week, he joined the Army. I put my arms around him and cried. Everyone was crying with me for Tom."

"Tom told us about what a wonderful family they were. His sister sounded like a terrific little girl. It wasn't long before everyone was telling each other about their wonderful families. Many of them told us that their family members were already looking forward to their coming home after the war was won. Lots of the stories were funny and people started smiling again."

"I soon had them all singing "God Bless America" and "Yes, Jesus Loves Me." Some of them had wonderful voices. I asked Tom Timmons if he would dance with me. He swung me around in the aisle and all the other men clapped. Soldiers from other train cars came to our car to see where the party was."

"They started giving me more money. I had never seen that much money before. There were a few bills and lots of change. Two of the men helped me carry it when I took it to put it into Mother's purse. Mother woke up when I was zipping her purse shut. When one of the men told Mother that they were helping me carry some money the men had given me, she was embarrassed and apologized. She sternly told me to sit down."

"Once Mother fell asleep, the soldiers in seats way up the aisle called me up to their seats. I talked to them about everything good that ever happened to me. I kissed them on the cheek and started turning somersaults in the aisle of the train until I got dizzy and sat down on the aisle floor laughing. Pretty soon I had so much money I took it to my mother's purse once more."

"Mother was still sound asleep so she didn't notice all the dollars, half dollars and quarters going into the purse. The purse was over half full on one side of the zipper."

"Men from other train cars asked me to come to their cars to entertain them as well. Altogether I visited four of the train cars. The soldiers in each train car knew about the others giving me money, so they tried to give me more than the others. Mother's purse was getting full."

"Many of the soldiers asked me to tell them more about what God had done for me and my family. I told them that I knew Jesus Christ died for my sins and their sins and would forgive them and me if we were sorry when we did something wrong. I told them that our Sunday school teacher told us that we needed to tell Him that we were sorry for what we had ever done and promise to trust Jesus to take care of us. I told them how nice my teacher was. Most of them said some of the things God did for our family were miracles. Some Christian men told stories about how Jesus had saved them or their family. Most all the men wanted to know everything they could about what God and Jesus wanted them to do."

"Everyone wanted their kiss on the cheek. The singing was beautiful when the men in four of the train cars stood up and met in two cars. When we all sang "God Bless America" together, most of the soldiers were crying. Someone called the conductor of the train and had him sing with us. He cried too."

"The train stopped at our destination in Ohio. Tom Timmons, the soldier whose seat was across the aisle from Mother and me, put me on his shoulders, and two others carried our luggage. They quickly walked Mother and me to the train station around the corner, where we had to catch another train."

"When Tom Timmons put me down, I smiled at him and kissed him. He smiled and said, 'Joyce, you sure do remind me of my little sister.' He had a tear in one eye."

"All three soldiers were crying when they thanked me for entertaining them when they were so lonely. I told them I'd pray for them and all the troops that were so nice to me on the train. One of them told Mother that he would pray for her brother if there was a war. Once again, I gave them hugs and kissed their cheeks. They hurried to return to their train before it left."

"Aunt Josephine and a neighbor were at the next Ohio train station to meet us. When we went inside Aunt Josephine's apartment, Mother said her shoulder hurt because her purse was so heavy. I told her it was probably all the money from the soldiers. Mother and Aunt Josephine wondered what I was talking about."

"When I explained how nice the men were just because I sang, prayed for them, and did somersaults and flip flops in the aisle, Josephine laughed while Mother unzipped her purse."

"What a surprise when the dollar bills and change poured onto Mother's lap. Aunt Josephine picked up quarters, half dollars, and silver dollars, while Mother stacked the dollar bills. She and Aunt Josephine started counting. Mother told me I had over three hundred dollars that I could put in my piggy bank when I got home. I told her, "No Mother. All the soldiers told me to give the money to you so that all of us could have a vacation and go to movies and restaurants."

"Let me tell you, we had a fun vacation! That evening, Uncle Bob went with us to a movie. We went to three movies altogether and shared two bags of popcorn and two large cokes at each movie. We bought lots of good food to eat at home."

"We went to the local radio station to a breakfast broadcast. Before they talked to anyone else, they interviewed Mother, Aunt Josephine, and me. The man in charge told us that we could be heard all over the United States. Aunt Josephine told him that she had called friends and family in Merrysville and they would be listening. It was pretty thrilling."

"We ate at some nice restaurants, and even got ice cream from the ice cream truck that passed her house every day."

"On the way home, Mother tried to stay awake, but couldn't. I'm embarrassed to tell you that I again entertained the troops. This time it was Marines and the Army Air Force. They were headed for a base on the other side of the country."

"When we were safely home, Bob helped me count my money. I put much more than two hundred dollars into my piggy bank. Mother and Dad were speechless since, as you all know, I was usually a shy kid. Bob said to me, 'I taught you and many others how to do the flip flops, but nobody ever gave me a dollar."

Joyce laughed and said, "There. That's my train story. Bob quickly said, "Not quite. You forgot something. Joyce felt bad for me and gave me five of the one-dollar bills. That made me happy. I gave a dollar to church and put three dollars in my bank. I used the other dollar to treat everyone to hot fudge sundaes." Joyce smiled at Bob and said, "You're right Bob."

"I forgot all about that. That was the first hot fudge sundae you and I ever ate. Wasn't it? I remember it was delicious." Bob confirmed that it was his first hot fudge sundae. When Bob stood up and started walking, everyone joined him.

Amanda was really shocked but loved Joyce's train story. She said, "Joyce, that was great. You were so shy then when I knew you. I never would have guessed you could have done that at that time. I imagine that Mother heard you on the radio if Josephine called her. I think it was wonderful. Just think, you were able to stay awake all night, on two different nights." Joyce wasn't sure if any of the boys, except for Bob,believed her.

Jimmy looked at Joyce and smiled. He spoke up and said, "You were asleep Amanda since you were only four, and it was early in the morning, but I was awake. Mother, Dad, and I listened to your interview at The Breakfast Club. Mr. Perkins and Dad talked about it with Mother. They were surprised when the man talked to you three for so long. When you came back home, our dads told your mother about what a good job you three did." Both girls looked at him and said, "Wow." Amanda didn't say anything, but she was mad at herself for not being awake to hear it.

Chapter 18

Birthdays

Amanda and Joyce's friend, named Abby, turned ten just twenty days before Joyce's birthday. Everyone at church and school felt sorry for Abby and her sister Sylvia because their parents died in a bad car accident. She and Sylvia lived with their grandparents since the accident.

Joyce told Amanda, "Some of my friends are jealous of Abby." Amanda was surprised and asked, "Why?" Joyce explained, "they said that Abby had told them that you considered her as your very best special friend. Ever since that time last month when I heard Abby tell Nellie something untrue about you and other friends, then pretended to be your best friend, I haven't trusted her. You and I have both seen Abby hurt people's feelings on purpose."

"I told the girls that you and I have lots of other friends, but you and I are best friends." Amanda nodded her head and said, "Thank you Joyce. I feel that way, too. I don't think we could call someone a special friend that would say some of those things Abby has said."

Joyce nodded and said, "I do think we should go to her birthday party though or most of our friends won't go." Amanda nodded. She let Joyce know that the friends who heard Abby talking about her and some of their other friends, asked Amanda if she and Joyce were still going.

Abby's grandparents gave her a shiny new bike at the fun birthday party they had for her. Every girl attending was amazed at the beautiful bike.

While most guests were ooh-ing and ah-ing, Abby's grandmother pulled Joyce aside and told her how much Sylvia loved the coat that she had given to her through the Salvation Army. Joyce told her that she was so glad that Sylvia was able to wear it, but she was embarrassed about why she gave away a coat that she had only worn once to school.

Joyce explained, "One day, late this winter, my brother Bob and I were playing near the creek, behind our big back yard on our way home. We hadn't been able to ice skate on it for several weeks. The creek had been frozen over for most of the winter but it was in the process of thawing. When I started walking out on it, Bob warned me, 'Joyce, you had better come back. It isn't solid, and you're going to fall through.' I gave him that look, and was quick to reply, 'No, I'm not. See? It's holding me.' Just to prove my point, I kept inching out, even though I could feel that the ice was rubbery."

"To my shocking surprise, everyone heard a noisy cracking sound, and in I went. A big splash! It was a good thing the water was only about eight inches deep. Of course, I wasn't wearing my old clothes that I normally wore when we played in that area. Wouldn't you know? I had on my brand-new snowsuit, the one I gave Sylvia. I immediately remembered that Mother had told me that morning to come right home and change my snow suit before I went out to play. I should not get into any deep snow with my brand-new snowsuit since it is a good grade of wool and would need to be dry cleaned if it got wet or dirty."

"Oh, I was so cold when I pushed myself up and out of the water. The coat and pants were soaked, and I didn't have any time to lose. I just knew Mother was going to scold me. I went crying, screaming, and freezing, back up the hill. I was sure that I saw Bob holding his hand over his mouth, and snickering. What could I say? After all, he had warned me. I had to prove my point. Mother was furious. I didn't blame her."

"Dad took my snowsuit. He was going to drop it off at the dry cleaners, but he had an appointment he had to keep. He couldn't get the snowsuit to the dry cleaners until the next day. By that time, it had shrunk. My punishment was no dinner, early to bed, and Mother wouldn't let me listen to Little Orphan Annie on the radio that night."

"I realized there was a lesson to learn from every setback. This one was, 'Sometimes it's wise to listen to your twin brother and not try to prove a point.' Bob could have said, "I told you so." But he didn't. He knew that I was already telling myself that I should have listened. He knew that I had never missed an episode of "Little Orphan Annie" before that day."

"Unfortunately, when the snowsuit was returned from the drycleaners, it had shrunk, and it wouldn't fit me. Only Mother saw me crying when she had me carry it into the Salvation Army store so someone could get some use out of it last winter. The receptionist told me, 'I'm sorry your snowsuit shrank so you couldn't wear it. It might make you feel better to know that a little girl and her grandmother came in a few hours ago because something happened to her snowsuit. I felt bad when I had to tell the little girl that we were out of snow suits. Her grandmother gave me her phone number and asked me to call if any snowsuit was brought in.'"

"When I heard her say grandmother, of course I thought of Sylvia. I asked if the little girl's name was Sylvia. When she said yes, that made me feel so much better. I doubt if I ever have a snowsuit that I liked as well as Sylvia's. I kept the snowsuit and told the Salvation Army lady that I'd personally deliver it to Sylvia. After I gave it to Sylvia, Mother took me to JC Penney's and found a nice-looking snowsuit on sale for two dollars. I knew it wasn't nearly as nice as the one that I had ruined by disobeying mother. When I saw Sylvia wearing the snowsuit at school a week later, I felt good."

"I knew that Sylvia's parents had been killed in an automobile accident one or two years ago. Everyone who knows her and Abby are so happy that you and their grandpa love them and take such good care of them."

"After that, I thanked God that Sylvia had a beautiful snowsuit and I felt grateful for my new snowsuit. It also taught me a lesson to listen when Mother tells me not to do something." Sylvia's grandmother smiled and gave Joyce a hug. Although she was smiling, Joyce saw a tear fall on the grandmother's cheek. Joyce was so glad that she and Amanda decided to attend Abby's birthday party.

At dinner that night, Joyce was still thinking about that shiny bike. Her dad asked her, "What are you thinking about Joyce?" She half-smiled and told him, "Nothing important really. It is just that Abby got a beautiful silver and black bicycle with a chrome back seat today. Her grandparents gave it to her at her birthday party. We all told her it is lovely."

"She asked Amanda and me to go biking with her since her sister doesn't have a bike. Amanda has her mother's old blue Schwinn bike; I'm not jealous, but it dawned on me that I don't have anything to go riding with them. Amanda told her we'd consider doing that sometime."

Joyce's dad didn't say anything, but the next day he bought a second-hand bike that needed fixing. He got it for only a dollar. Restoring things was his specialty, so he worked on it in his workshop. He tore it all down, sanded it, soaked the screws, nuts, and bolts to clean them, and repainted the bicycle frame with two coats of shiny blue paint. He put two fancy white stripes with a swirl of paint on the fenders. It was beautiful, and totally different from anything you could buy.

He bought new blue hand grips and seat for it. The hand grips had nice long blue and white streamers that made it look classy. The day he finished it was Joyce's tenth birthday. When he gave it to Joyce at her birthday party on Saturday morning, Joyce was one proud daughter. She smiled and told Abby that she would love to go bicycle riding with her and Amanda whenever it was OK with Amanda's and her parents. That pleased Abby.

Joyce knew her dad loved her a lot to take the time and effort to redo that bike for her. In front of everyone at her birthday party, she threw her arms around her dad's neck, gave him a big kiss, and said, "Thank you Daddy for all your hard work. It's so-o-o beautiful!"

"It means so much to me because of all the love and work you put into it. You're the greatest!" Everyone clapped and went over to look at the bike. Each guest commented that it was the most beautiful bike she had ever seen. Even Abby agreed.

Except for Joyce's mother, no one noticed the tear in the corner of her dad's eye. From her girlfriends, Joyce received some beautiful paper dolls, a dress for her favorite doll, a necklace, and the book "Little Women". Joyce couldn't have been happier. After the party, Joyce, Amanda, and Abby rode their bikes often.

Saturday afternoon was Bob's birthday party. He was so excited because his favorite gift was the expensive microscope that he had wanted for two years. It was a joint gift from his parents and his four grandparents. The party guests gave him airplane models and fishing items. Bob knew that he would be looking for bugs and many other things to see under that magnificent microscope. What a great birthday the twins had. It felt great to be ten years old and going into the sixth grade.

Chapter 19

Heat Wave

What a heat wave Indiana was experiencing! The radio announcer said it was a new record. The old record of ninety plus degrees for seven straight days was in 1905. As Iris Belle was wiping the sweat off her brow, she wished she could go to Alaska. Then she remembered that last night the radio announcer reported that it was hot in Juneau, Alaska. Her family and all their friends found it hard to sleep in the stifling heat. Their electric fans just didn't cool the bedrooms.

Joyce and Amanda made sure to go over to the barn at least once a day. For some reason, the barn was much cooler than their houses. Yesterday and today, they went twice. Both times they filled the water troughs for the cats, chickens and roosters with the cold water that came from the faucets upstairs and down.

Last month, Mr. Andy told the boys and girls that the ice-cold water came from a deep well under the barn. He showed them the door near the bathroom in the office. He said those were the steps that went down to the well, but he had the only key and kept it locked.

Mr. Andy told the kids that there has never been any problem with the well or pump but they learned about an experience he once had in the well with his dad. "There were snakes and huge spiders all around the walls of the top ten steps going down. Of course, the water is pumped from the bottom of the well so it is not unsafe."

"Once a year, I have a person from the Health Department go down and check the water. It always tests good. However, no one from the Health Department is willing to go down more than once." The thought of those first ten steps of the well put goose pimples on all the children's arms.

No one ever considered trying to unlock that door. Both girls thought Mr. Andy was just teasing them and their friends. They felt pretty sure that there had never been a snake in there, but they never told the boys what they thought. They loved the well water, and often splashed it on their heads or their faces. The chickens, cats and roosters gave them a strange look when they did it.

With the blistering heatwave hitting the country, it was a bad time for anyone without an air conditioner to have company. In 1946, most people didn't have air conditioners.

Iris Belle's only sister, Josephine, and her four-year old daughter, Julie Mae, surprised the family when they stopped by for two days on their way to Upper Michigan to visit her sister-in-law. Josephine's husband was deep sea fishing with friends off the Florida coast, so she took this opportunity to visit from their home in Ohio.

Yesterday, Art Perkins, had ordered the largest window air conditioner that was available. It would barely fit in their living room window. The family planned to sleep in that room at night during the summer.

"Thank you, God, in only three more hours that wonderful air conditioner is going to be delivered and installed!" Iris Belle told Art how much she was looking forward to the temperature tomorrow morning when they awoke. She yawned as she slowly got out of the bed. The sheet was wet from their perspiration over the last seven hours.

The cool shower she took helped for a short time, but the heat really bothered her. She didn't plan to cook until the weather changed. Art told her last night, "We are going to eat every meal out in a nice cool restaurant while your sister and niece are here."

Her sister couldn't have come at a worse time because of the Perkins' schedule. When Iris Belle looked at her calendar schedule yesterday, she discovered that the large church bake sale was scheduled for tomorrow.

This meant today was going to be a busy day because she had promised to bake two pies and two cakes for the bake sale. She smiled at the thought of having the cool living room to enjoy while the kitchen, with the oven and fan going, would be miserable.

Josephine came into the kitchen, searching for Julie Mae. Iris Belle heard her say, "Julie Mae isn't in Joyce's room. Have you seen her?" Iris Belle hadn't seen her since last night. Josephine called, "Julie Mae, where are you Darling?"

In her mind, Iris Belle was considering what she needed to start her hot task when she opened her pantry door. Both Iris Belle and Josephine let out a scream. Joyce came running in to see what happened. There sat her four-year-old cousin, Julie Mae, dripping wet with sweat, with a big smile on her face.

She was so delighted with what she was doing for Iris Belle that she put her hands up as she told her audience, "Look, Mommy. I'm helping to bake cakes. Look Aunt Iris Belle, I bake cakes too."

In front of Joyce and the two sisters was the open suitcase for Joyce's doll clothes, with some doll clothes still visible under the mess. Nearly empty sacks of flour, brown sugar, Morton's salt, and opened cans of all the spices from the spice rack were strewn on the floor at Julie Mae's feet, evidence of what was in the suitcase on the doll clothes.

Half of the cooking chocolate was still in Julie Mae's hand. Some of the chocolate, not in the suitcase, appeared to be dripping out of her mouth. Joyce and Iris Belle felt like crying but found themselves laughing as they were sitting on the floor beside Julie Mae. Iris Belle gave her young niece a hug, smiled, and got up to make a telephone call. Josephine was still sitting in a daze.

When her friend from church answered her call, Iris Belle told her everything that she had experienced that morning. She suggested the summer church bake sale scheduled for tomorrow be postponed until after the heat passed; otherwise, she had to count Iris Belle out. No baking at her house until the temperature was livable. Her friend agreed. Within thirty minutes, she received three phone calls from church members who thanked her for getting the bake sale postponed. Everyone had a great laugh when they heard about Julie Mae's eagerness to help with the bake sale.

That morning, Josephine was busy washing doll clothes, Joyce's suitcase, and Julie Mae's shorts and top. As the air conditioner was being installed, the two sisters went shopping to replace spices and baking items.

When they looked in a restaurant window, they saw the delicious-looking pies inside. They stepped into the air-conditioned restaurant to cool off and have some pie ala mode with glasses of cold milk. Sitting in a cool room, eating yummy pie and ice cream was such a delight for the two sisters. Josephine apologized for her young daughter's activities, and Iris Belle reminded her of the cowboys' and Indians' incident that happened years ago when Josephine was babysitting with her children. Josephine told about their mother's shocked reaction when she was told the story. The two sisters commented that their mother no longer bought costumes for their children.

While they were gone, Joyce, Amanda, and Julie Mae ran through the sprinkler in the shade under Amanda's large oak tree. When Joyce and Amanda returned from going into the bathroom at Joyce's house, Julie Mae had disappeared. So had the sprinkler.

The girls ran around the corner and there was Julie Mae holding the hose gushing with water. Somehow, Julie Mae had removed the sprinkler. Joyce took the hose and shut off the water. She asked Julie Mae what she was doing with the hose. Julie Mae had a big smile on her face as she enthusiastically told Joyce, "I put gasoline in Uncle Art's truck."

The girls ran to the truck and sure enough, there was a trail of the water from the hose to the gas tank. Fortunately for Art and the girls, all his trucks had locks on their gas tanks, so no water had gone into the gas tank.

Both girls said, "Thank you God!"

That evening, the family returned from eating at an air-conditioned restaurant. Cool air greeted them when they opened the door. They realized they would not have to sleep on sheets on the living room floor; the air conditioner had cooled the bedrooms considerably. What a pleasant surprise. Josephine and Iris Belle took Julie Mae and the kids down to the basement for the rest of the evening. They knew that if they stayed upstairs with the wonderful new air conditioner, Julie Mae would find many new areas that she could explore, to nobody's appreciation.

Josephine waited until her creative, ambitious, healthy daughter was sound asleep before she carried her up to the bedroom that was pleasantly cooled by the air conditioner. The next morning, family members had breakfast with Josephine and Julie Mae before they were safely in their car and on their way to visit Josephine's husband's family in Michigan.

When she kissed everyone goodbye, Julie Mae told them she was on her way to help her aunt do some baking. Joyce and Iris Belle were pleased to see that Julie Mae had not done anything helpful that morning while they were eating breakfast.

A few minutes later, when the girls were in the hot car with Betty Martin, Joyce and Amanda talked about doing a good deed for someone in July. They laughed and talked about all the fun they had in June picking Mrs. Hall's black raspberries before their trip. The girls were happy to ride with Betty to take twenty-six jars of black raspberry jam and twenty-two jars of black raspberry jelly to Mrs. Hall.

Mrs. Hall cried and told Betty and the girls how surprised she was that her berries filled four boxes of these pint-size jars of jam and jelly. She was sincere when she said she was pleased and surprised that she received all the pies that she and her neighbors enjoyed that summer. Everyone was hugged and kissed.

Betty didn't tell her then, but during the next month Mrs. Hall would receive several pies made from the black raspberry bushes in the Martin orchards. Jam and jelly made from Martin Orchard berries would go on the shelves in their basement because their family also liked jam or jelly with their peanut butter sandwiches.

Chapter 20

Cops and Robbers

With tennis lessons, home chores, and so much work in the gardens, Joyce and Amanda hardly ever had the chance to go to the barn during the week. On an early Wednesday morning, the girls took their breakfast and headed for the barn to eat in the hideout before it was too warm. They planned to be there for about an hour.

The 8:40 a.m. train was thirty minutes early when the girls heard its whistle. Minutes later they realized the train was at the large overhead water tank, filling up with water.

The girls looked out of their secret window. Three men got off the train, walked down the track, and spotted the barn. The girls had planned to be out of there before the train came, but now they couldn't safely leave.

They lay quietly on their blanket and listened. The three men were rude and used bad language. The girls had never heard many of the words. The men's conversation made it clear that they had come to town to perform a robbery, but on the pretense of getting a job. Their plan, however, was to put their applications in at every business, using fake names and information.

Their goal was to rob the Building and Loan on Friday after all the businesses made their deposits, just an hour before the money would be picked up by the armored truck. The girls were concerned about the evil way they laughed when they were rehearsing their plan. One of the men, with a bad scar on his forehead, snickered as he said, "I can hardly wait to shock employees of this village."

"What a surprise when they realize they were held up by city slickers." One of the other men laughed an evil laugh then said, "I wonder what Mr. High and Mighty will tell our sister about this robbery, next Sunday." All three men thought that was funny.

Another of the men said two or three customers were paying off their mortgages earlier that day. The bad, rude, men planned to go into the Building and Loan on the pretense of depositing money. They would wait until after the office was empty except for the manager and one teller. They would tie up the employees and take the money.

An out-of-state car would pick them up at the back door of the Building and Loan. They had been told that a Board member said it was going to be easy. The girls were shocked to hear who the informer was supposed to be. The men were only there for about thirty minutes when they decided to go check out the village for a hot breakfast.

The girls waited until they were sure the men were gone before they hurried home. When Betty Martin saw them coming, she called Iris Belle and asked her to come over because she could tell that their daughters had a problem. When the girls ran into the house, both mothers knew something was very wrong. The girls appeared to be in denial of the information they had heard.

They told their mothers everything they heard and about the sarcastic attitude of the men. The men said they knew about how easy it was going to be to rob the Building and Loan because of a Board member, Mr. Spitznaugle. Like their daughters, neither mother could believe the accusation. Amanda questioned whether they should call Mr. Spitznaugle or the sheriff.

Everyone knew that only the sheriff would be able to safely arrest the men when they were making the robbery attempt. The sheriff was quick to agree that he didn't believe it was true. He also knew that the robbery had to be stopped. He suggested that Mr. Spitznaugle should not be involved in any way.

The sheriff now had a good relationship with the manager of the Building and Loan. After all, the manager thought the sheriff, on his own, had solved the mystery of the Building and Loan robberies just weeks ago.

He met with him personally and explained that it had come to his attention that a robbery of the Building and Loan was planned and that a current Board member was reported to know about it.

When he told the manager what the three men supposedly knew about what was going to happen on Friday, the manager knew that this threat was real. He also knew that this information had to have been shared by a Board member who was at last week's Board meeting. He promised that he would not share anything to anyone about the sheriff's plan to capture the crooks in the act of robbing.

Four employees of the sheriff's office would be sitting in the private Board room from noon until they arrested the robbers. The robbers did not know any of the sheriff's employees, nor the employees of the Building and Loan. When the last known customer was out of the Building and Loan, the employees would trade places with the deputies.

The Sheriff's cars would be hidden in the Martin barn, less than a block away. A lookout would be on the second floor of the barn. He would be able to see the front and back doors of the Building and Loan. The lookout would watch for the three men to enter the front door of the Building and Loan. He would also watch to see a car drive around to the alley and park by the back door of the Building and Loan, then dispatch the Sheriff Department cars to that area.

The deputies would drive their cars to enter the same alley in both directions. They would capture the driver and anyone else in the robbers' car. Another deputy would pull up in front of the Building and Loan once the robbers were inside. The sheriff and his staff would arrest the men as soon as they started to draw their guns. It was going to take twelve of the Sheriff's staff to do this safely and swiftly.

In the meantime, none of the Sheriff's cars would be seen in Merrysville so the three men would not recognize anyone. Their cars would be put into the Martin barn very early in the morning. Betty was happy to volunteer to have enough food for the deputies in the refrigerator and stove in the office of the huge barn. She could hardly wait to plan the meals.

Sure enough, the three men spent an hour or two every morning and afternoon looking for work. For the three days they were in town they stayed away from the Building and Loan.

On Friday, three loans were paid off, all by check. Those checks, and the small amount of cash received by the Building and Loan, were put into a large safe with a lock set to open when the armored truck was scheduled to arrive. This was done on every Friday afternoon, twenty minutes before closing time. Many of the Board members were unaware of this precaution that had taken place since the office opened years ago.

The deputy spotted a car stopping in front of the door of the Building and Loan. He alerted the teams to get into their cars. When the three men walked into the Building and Loan, the car quickly drove to the alley behind the door of the Building and Loan. It took less than three minutes for the barn doors to open and the woman driving the car to be arrested.

The three men saw there were no customers in the lobby, so they entered the main door and two of them pulled out a gun and ordered the man behind the counter to gather up all the cash and turn it over.

One robber started to go behind the counter to tie up the employees. The man hadn't moved the rope in his hand when he was surprised by the sheriff. He stepped out behind a door, and quickly handcuffed the robber. The deputies in the car that just pulled into the front parking lot were already inside, behind the robbers.

They joined three of the sheriff's staff who had already arrested the other two men, taken their guns and handcuffed their hands behind their backs. The Sheriff went to the back door and had his deputies bring in the handcuffed driver of the out-of-state car. The driver was a woman who was screaming bad language to the three men she knew. They were still in a state of shock.

Seconds later, the Building and Loan employee was locking the front door. After the CLOSED sign was turned, everyone was sitting in the locked Board Room.

Andy Spitznaugle was driving back to his office at the end of the workday. He noticed all the Sheriff's vehicles around the Building and Loan. It was past closing time. He needed to see what was wrong. When he unlocked the front door and went inside, the business area was empty. He quickly relocked the door.

Andy heard an interrogation taking place in the Board Room. He didn't go into the room but was shocked when he heard the hysterical woman telling her story. When he realized what had happened, he had to smile. The woman and three men that asked him about a job yesterday, came to town to rob this Building and Loan.

Andy couldn't believe what he was hearing. When being interrogated, the four told the sheriff that Andy Spitznaugle let them know about how easy it would be to rob the Building and Loan before the money was picked up.

The woman screamed at the men, "What dumb thing did you do or say for this to happen?" She told the sheriff that she had visited a church last Sunday. The church served a delicious hot meal on Sundays after church. Last Sunday was the first time she had come and attended the service, before mealtime. She listened to the message by Pastor Spitznaugle.

That pastor told his church audience that he had talked to his dad, Andy Spitznaugle, on Saturday night. The pastor told of his dad's businesses and that he was a Board member of a busy Building and Loan in Merrysville, Indiana. He proudly gave an example of the coming week and how successful it was.

The dishonest woman told the Sheriff she had heard Pastor Spitznaugle tell the congregation how proud he was, not only of his dad but also the citizens of Merrysville, Indiana. The pastor told how his family had donated the land for the park, schools, and churches. The congregation learned how the pastor's grandparents and parents began the village over 50 years ago.

She said she called her three brothers and told them about how easy she thought it should be to go into that small village and come out rich from robbing the Building and Loan. She never gave it a thought that most people might pay off their loan with a check.

When Andy called his son after the attempted robbery, Andy realized that his son, the minister, was proud when he heard his father was elected a member of the Building and Loan Board. He learned that his son had mentioned robberies and hold-ups at larger facilities, but proudly said that could not happen in Merrysville because of their safety and security.

Andy decided at that moment to be more careful when he shared anything about this village with his children. His son told him that he had shared with his congregation all that his family had done for the village.

The Sheriff confidentially told Andy that the girls had heard the men talking at the barn. The sheriff assured him that he and the girls knew this attempted robbery had nothing to do with him.

Meanwhile, the Sheriff's deputies drove the four attempted robbers to the County Jail. Their car was later sold at an auction.

Chapter 21

SUNDAY FUN TIME

It was raining on Sunday; after church and dinner, no one wanted to play checkers or a board game. Chris reminded the kids that Mr. Andy had encouraged them to play in his barn when it rained. Amanda said, "Let's do it." Jimmy made a phone call to another friend from church and shared their plan.

Betty Martin, Jimmy and Amanda's mother, knew the kids would be hungry before the evening youth meeting. She sent a large loaf of homemade bread, jars of peanut butter and jelly, her famous cinnamon rolls, jelly rolls, and a canister of iced lemonade with the children.

The kids grabbed umbrellas and ran to meet their friends over at the barn. The roosters greeted them, noisily but friendly, as they came down the road. The boys insisted the reason the roosters were crowing nicely was because they talked to the roosters whenever they passed the barn.

The boys never bothered to mention that when they were alone, the roosters' voices and glares were menacing. In unison, the girls smiled as they answered, "Thank you boys!" Joyce and Amanda looked at each other and nodded.

Chris pointed to the geese and ducks that were swimming in the rain. There were many baby and young ducks of all ages following their mothers and dads. The rain convinced the kids to get inside and play something in there. Two boys drew a hopscotch board and two shuffleboard courts on the smooth cement floor. The other boys went out in the rain and brought in sticks and flat rocks to use for the games. Everyone had a great time as they played many games.

At five o'clock, everyone sat on the floor where they talked and ate. Jimmy laughed when he heard each kid was convinced that he or she was the winner today. He declared that he was going to bring paper and pencils the next time they came to keep score. Everyone laughed.

Afterward, everyone helped sweep the floor so there would be no crumbs to draw mice or rats to the barn. The kids always had a sack in their backpack to remove all the crumbs from the barn.

One of the boys found a basketball in the corner. Everyone played a quick game of twenty-one, so they could practice their free throws. Like every male in Indiana, all the boys dreamed of someday becoming a famous basketball player. To the boys disappointment, Joyce and Amanda scored more baskets than their brothers.

When the children realized it was time to go back to church, they grabbed their umbrellas and were ready to head in that direction. As Jimmy was opening the door, Mr. Andy drove behind the barn to feed his animals. When he came into the barn, he was pleased to learn that the children had spent the day there and had cleaned the floor so nicely.

The boys helped Mr. Andy bring in the supplies, and then all the children left to go to church together. On the way to church, Amanda suggested that all of them hide behind the pews just as soon as they arrived. When they saw Mr. Andy coming behind the pew, they could jump out and say, "BOO!" All the kids thought that would be so much fun. They ran as fast as they safely could in the rain. They arrived at the church less than ten minutes before church started.

Even though the children had run all the way, they were greeted inside by Mr. Andy, who was wearing his big smile. The kids laughed because they knew he did it to surprise them. They loved his sense of humor.

After evening church, Mr. Andy returned to the barn and fed his animals. He had a smile on his face when he remembered how surprised the kids were to see him there. He was pleased that he was going to be their Sunday school teacher in September.

Chapter 22

FAMILY SHARING TIME

Iris Belle Perkins was attending a large women's retreat with Betty Martin. The women were staying overnight at the church in another city and were expected to be home late Saturday evening. The weather had turned from very hot on Thursday to cool and raining all day today. After Friday afternoon dinner, Art Perkins and his children sat around the table and talked. Bob and Joyce were talking about the Land and Water Sports event coming up in several weeks. Two weeks after that event, would be a weekend Tennis Tournament.

Mr. Andy had told Amanda and Joyce that he was looking forward to seeing the tennis match between the two girls vs. Iris Belle Perkins and Betty Martin. "He remembered that Mother and Mrs. Martin are excellent players. He thinks we girls are getting competitive. He believes it will be an even match."

"Bob, since you and Jimmy have only been practicing for a few weeks, Amanda and I are predicting that you are going to get smeared by Dad and Mr. Martin." Bob told his dad and Joyce that he and Jimmy were practicing every time they saw an open tennis court. He said the two of them are going to the courts right after they finished working in the field, instead of going fishing. Joyce laughed and said, "I hope you're able to find an empty court often. Every time we go past you two practicing alone, it makes us feel more than just a little happy with our progress."

©Annabelle Sandlin

The day before, Iris Belle Perkins laughed and told the kids, "Well, Betty and I have been practicing with Mr. Andy, of course. We have also been practicing every chance we can. We really want to be prepared."

Art Perkins frowned and cleared his throat. He looked at Bob and told him, "You and Jimmy probably have a better chance at beating Mr. Martin and me than we have of beating you. Mr. Andy told me that, as of right now, your sisters have a chance of wiping out your mother and Mrs. Martin. Your mother and I still need to use every available opportunity to practice."

Mr. Perkins continued, "We need to bring our playing above 'good enough' so we don't embarrass our families at the tennis match. Mr. Andy told me on Sunday that the Summer Sports Week games last year were so good that he expects a crowd of at least four thousand people this year."

"He announced that the tennis competition, two weeks later, has many players registered. There will be players from six Indiana counties and a few teams from out of state. He is concerned about where everyone can park for the Tennis Tournament Weekend. The Village Council will be talking about the parking problem in their next meeting."

"Joyce asked when the dates of the events will be made public. Art Perkins told his children, "Mr. Andy will make a special announcement next week at the Wednesday night movie downtown. He has received confirmation that NBC Sports will be sending a camera truck and several of their employees to tape the events of this year's Summer Sports Week in Merrysville. He and the committee wanted to make sure the events would coordinate when the NBC Sports team could come."

"Ever since NBC Sports began on May 17, 1939, it has been the dream of our village to create an event that would attract them to come here. Some of the events will be broadcasted on their radio programs. Many will be shown in movie theaters as a trailer to the movie."

"Our village committee has invited NBC Sports to cover the tennis games as well. Mr. Andy hopes they will be interested. Merrysville will be notified in about two weeks if they are."

"President Truman and national news networks are trying to encourage small towns and large cities, to get their kids to exercise, as well as to include their youth in healthy competition." A look of utter terror crossed Bob's face. Bob promised that he and Jimmy would take their responsibility more seriously since they would be representing Merrysville, as well as their families, especially on national radio.

Bob asked, "Did you and Mother even hear about the canoe jousting at the Summer Sports Week last year? I don't remember if Joyce or I told you about our experience. It was when Mother joined you on your two-week training session. Joyce and I stayed with the Martin family." Mr. Perkins shook his head and said he wasn't aware that there was such a thing as canoe jousting. He asked what happened.

Bob and Joyce were all smiles when Bob told him, "The committee for the event decided at the last moment to get some canoes and add the sport for boys and girls."

"All participants had to be good swimmers. The competition was two girls (or boys) in one canoe competing with two girls (or boys) in another canoe. One girl rowed while the other one stood up with a soft rubber oar. The goal is to knock the person in the other canoe into the water."

"Jimmy Martin and I signed up for the boys' event. Amanda talked Joyce into entering as well for the girls. After many jousting eliminations, the four of us were the semi-finalists for our age groups."

"Joyce dodged a fast oar and struck her 12-year-old competitor on her legs and 'PLOP'. Joyce and Amanda were the champions for girls of all ages."

"Very surprised champions, I might add," Joyce laughed.

Bob continued, "Jimmy had easily won every one of our contests. He was great as a jouster. Jimmy is good at rowing but he didn't have any experience in maneuvering a canoe."

"We had been told the boys we were competing with were young boys visiting from Indianapolis. I felt pretty smug; like a young city boy from Indianapolis was no competition for Jimmy and me. I'm almost as tall as Jimmy is. I suggested that I would like to do the jousting for the Boys Grand Championship since I had rowed all the other times. It was fine with Jimmy. Of course, my thinking was a mistake. Bad thinking."

"I can tell you that my inexperience as a jouster was recognized as soon as I stood up and took the oar. An unexpected problem! I had forgotten to look to see who my competition was. I was expecting an eight- or nine-year-old boy. The boy standing in the other canoe didn't look like a city boy from Indianapolis; he looked like a giant. He was listed as twelve-years old; but looked as big as a 14 or 16-year-old." Joyce laughed and said, "Dad, he was a lot bigger than you." Bob nodded and continued, "One 'whap', and I was swimming to shore. Boys Grand Championship lost."

"The final Grand Championship was to be determined by jousting of the champions of the girls' and boys' events. Since Amanda was terrific at rowing, she rowed around the other canoe before stopping where the competition was to start. She carefully watched the jouster in the other canoe. She is very observant. She took notice of how the giant had his feet planted on the canoe bottom. I felt good when I saw her smile at Joyce."

"The 12-year-old giant, who had quickly put me into the water, seemed to be more than twice Joyce's size. He looked so smug when he saw how short Joyce was next to him. I think everyone watching was disgusted when he and the boy rowing, snickered. It reminded me of David and Goliath." Joyce laughed and said, "That's funny. It did me too."

Bob continued, "Amanda was an expert at rowing. She outfoxed the 12-year-old boy who was rowing Joyce's opponent. She had told Joyce to be alert, but to wait until she quickly stopped and swerved before she placed the first low blow."

"The opponent swung high, and Joyce ducked. Joyce 'whapped' the giant's legs as Amanda swerved. He didn't have a chance. Ker-splash! In he went."

"Since he fell into their canoe, the girls were wetter than the opponent who had rowed the loser. What a surprise it was to the crowd. Everyone sitting in the crowd stood up and cheered. I was proud of the girls."

Joyce spoke up, "Thank you Bob. Amanda and I found it hard to believe when we rowed to the official winners' corner and received the prize. Our hair was wetter than our swimsuits."

Bob laughed when he told Art, "The Grand Champion prize was a ten-dollar gift certificate from Miss Barnes. Mr. and Mrs. Martin joined the four of us. The girls were generous with their prize; they ordered hamburgers, French fries, and milkshakes for all of us. The next day, they treated us to delicious banana splits. With the few pennies left from the prize money, Amanda laughed and used them to buy six bubble gum balls, one for each of us from the machine by the cash register." Joyce laughed and said, "Ten dollars well spent." Bob nodded and said, "We were all winners."

Art couldn't keep from laughing as he tried to picture the events of that day. Art asked his twins, "Are you going to compete this year?" His kids looked at each other and shrugged their shoulders. Bob suddenly remembered something. He reminded his dad, "I just happened to think that you and Mom might be gone this year at the time of the Land and Water Sports event or the Tennis Championships."

Bob said, "Mr. Andy reported that so many people have signed up for the tennis tournaments that there will be a special weekend set aside for that activity. He is expecting several thousand people to participate."

Both kids said, at the same time, "Oh no! Come to think of it, will you two be here to play tennis against us? If not, we'll have to play two other adults." Art had neglected to tell the family that the annual meeting was going to be two weeks early this summer. He and Iris Belle would be home for both events. Art could hardly wait to watch his twins in action on the water. He didn't feel as good about the tennis matches.

What a nice time the children had getting to share the day with their dad. They had much to look forward to that summer in 1946.

Bob looked up at Joyce and his dad. Bob told them that their friends were going to participate in games at the park on the 4th of July. Joyce looked surprised and said, "Hey, we need to talk to our friends and see if there is something special we can do after the games. We've already heard Ellis and his singers who will entertain that evening before the fireworks."

The phone rang in Art's office. He looked at his watch. He told the kids, "Excuse me. I know who that is. It is a business call so I may be on the phone a long time."

Bob told him, "Please talk as long as you want, Dad. Amanda and Jimmy are in our driveway, coming toward the front porch. We know they're going to bring lots of good ideas about 4th of July evening plans. We'd love to have you join us when you're free."

Art said, "I'd love to join you four later." He went into his office to answer his phone call while Bob headed toward the front door.

THE END...

70% of royalties from "**The Barn That Crowed**" series will be donated to charities.

The remaining 30%
of royalties will be
used for publishing
and marketing books.

ABOUT THE AUTHOR

Annabelle Sandlin was born in New Richmond, Indiana, during an ice storm. Because her father couldn't drive the car over the ice, the doctor drove his horse and surrey to deliver baby Annabelle at home. As the youngest of six children, Annabelle often sat around the family dinner table telling stories. One person would start the story and then each family member would add a paragraph until they were able to bring the story to an end. Naturally this is how Annabelle thinks of her life; in chapters of various sizes that all weave the story of her life.

There are so many chapters to the book: loving people and life, time at church and in prayer, zany travel adventures and so much more. Annabelle has taken numerous cruises, traveled to forty-nine states. (Sorry, North Dakota), and visited forty-five countries and islands. She has taken great photographs from the wheelchair lift on Dave's van, helicopters, hot air balloons, planes, or lying on her back to get great shots of lighthouses, Notre Dame gargoyles, and many other positions needed to get unusual shots.

The most important chapter in Annabelle's book of life is family. Annabelle has two daughters and one son. She has also been blessed with three granddaughters, two grandsons, and one great-granddaughter. Her fondest memories center on her family.

To be in God's will for her life has always been Annabelle's greatest desire.

www.ingramcontent.com/pod-product-compliance
Lightning Source LLC
Chambersburg PA
CBHW040833010826
48978CB00012BB/740